그림에 관해 알아야 할 것들

Things to Know about Paintings

DARAKWON

About Wise & Wide

- 렉사일 지수(Lexile® measures)에 맞춘 체계적인 6단계 영어 독서 프로그램
- 우리나라와 세계의 초등 교과 과정을 분석해 뽑은 다채롭고 흥미로운 주제
- 스토리, 설명문, 명작 리라이팅 등 다양한 형식의 새롭고 유익한 읽을거리
- 정보와 재미, 논픽션 학습과 픽션 학습의 장점을 한 번에!
- 탄탄한 독후 활동으로 쑥쑥 자라는 사고력

Wise & Wide는 렉사일 지수(Lexile® measures)를 기준으로 각 단계를 체계적으로 나눈, 총 60권 구성의 6단계 영어 독서 프로그램입니다. 렉사일 지수는 미국 정규 공교육 과정과 여러 영어 프로그램에서 가장 많이 사용되는 영어 독서 지수입니다. 미국 50개 주 가운데 21개 주에서 렉사일 지수를 학기말 시험(End of Grade) 성적표에 직접 표시하며, 세계적으로 저명한 300개 이상의 출판사들이 렉사일 지수를 채택하여 사용하고 있기도 합니다. 우리나라와 미국, 영국, 호주 등 세계 초등 교과 과정을 분석해 뽑은 흥미로운 주제로 미국, 영국의 우수한 작가들이 집필한 다양한 종류의 읽을거리를 만나보세요. 도표(organizer) 완성, 자기 생각 말하기, 독후 테스트 풀기 등 탄탄한 독후 활동도 준비되어 있습니다.

시리즈 수준 & 렉사일 지수

시리즈 단계	렉사일 지수	미국 학년 (U.S. Grade)
Level 1	200L 이하	Pre K - K
Level 2	190L - 400L	Lower Grade 1
Level 3	350L - 530L	Upper Grade 1
Level 4	420L - 650L	Grade 2
Level 5	520L - 940L	Grade 3 - 4
Level 6	830L - 1070L	Grade 5 - 6

* 똑똑한 영어 읽기 Wise & Wide 시리즈의 1단계는 미국의 미취학 수준에 해당합니다.

* 렉사일 지수와 미국 학년과의 관계 출처: CCSS(Common Core State Standards) FOR ENGLISH LANGUAGE ARTS, APPENDIX A (2012, 미국 45개 주에서 사용 중)

퍼즐처럼 다양한 Topic List

	Level 1	Level 2	Level 3	Level 4	Level 5	Level 6
1 권	과학〉생물: 동물들의 겨울잠 Story	과학〉생물: 생물과 무생물 Story	과학〉생물〉 동물, 환경: 해달 Story	환경〉 자연과 인생: 해녀 & 감나무 Story	과학〉생물〉 동물: 아마존의 놀라운 동물들 Story	과학〉생물: 세균, 전염성 질환 Story
2 권	문학〉세계 명작: 이솝 우화 Story	문학〉전래 동화: 돌에 관한 옛이야기 Story	사회〉경제: 용돈 버는 사업, 저축 Story	과학〉생물〉 식물: 광합성 Story	과학〉지구과학: 지각, 지진, 화산, 대기 Report	수학〉수열: 황금 비율과 피보나치 수열 Story
3 권	과학〉물리: 그림자의 원리 Story	문학〉세계 명작: 피터 팬 Story	과학〉과학 기술: 나노봇 Story	문학〉신화: 세계의 천지 창조 이야기 Story	문학〉전설: 아서왕 이야기 Story	문학〉신화: 별자리 신화 Story
4 권	문학〉전래 문학: 탈무드 Story	과학〉생물〉 동물: 북극곰 Story	과학〉생물〉 동물: 마운틴 고릴라 Story	사회〉인류 문화: 세계의 놀라운 고대 문화 Story	과학〉지구과학: 구름과 날씨 Story	문학〉 인간과 동물: 소녀와 말의 우정 Story
5 권	사회〉윤리: 생활 속의 규범 Story	과학〉생물: 몸의 감각 Report	사회〉인류 문화: 세계의 독특한 축제 Report	예술〉음악: 오페라 이야기 Story	사회〉세계 문화· 역사: 르네상스 시대의 특징 Story	스포츠〉 보드 스포츠: 서핑 & 스노보딩 Story
6 권	사회〉세계지리, 여행: 세계의 명소 Story	과학〉생물〉 동물: 공룡 Story	과학〉천문학: 우주, 태양계 행성 Story	사회〉인물: 고난을 이겨낸 세 위인들 Story	과학〉과학 기술: 놀라운 로봇의 세계 Report	예술〉음악: 낭만주의 시대의 작곡가들 Report
7 권	과학〉우주 과학: 우주 비행사들의 생활 Report	사회〉인류 문화: 세계의 전설 속 괴물들 Report	수학〉기초 수학: 숫자, 측정, 형태, 데이터 Report	과학·사회〉 기술, 문화: 세계의 발명품 Report	예술〉미술: 세계의 명화 Report	사회〉인간과 동물: 인간을 위해 활약 하는 동물들 Report
8 권	사회〉인류 문화: 세계의 다양한 생활 문화 Story	예술〉음악: 오케스트라의 악기들 Story	사회〉생활 안전: 조난 시 기본 대처 방법 Story	사회〉역사: 미국의 골드러시 Report	사회·과학〉 심리학: 생활 속의 심리학 Story	문학〉세계 명작: 베니스의 상인 Story
9 권	사회〉직업: 여러 직업에 관한 인터뷰 Report	과학〉과학 기술: 시대의 변화와 기술의 발달 Story	사회〉정치〉선거: 학생회장 선거 Story	문학〉세계 명작: 셜록 홈즈 이야기 Story	문학〉세계 명작: 15소년 표류기 Story	사회〉역사·인물: 역사 속의 리더들 Report
10 권	문학〉전래 동화: 같은 주제의 동·서양 옛이야기 Story	스포츠〉겨울 스포 츠: 동계 올림픽 종목의 이모저모 Report	문학〉세계 명작: 오 헨리 단편 Story	스포츠〉구기 종목: 인기 있는 구기 종목의 이모저모 Report	사회〉역사: 역사를 뒤바꾼 세계사의 명장면 Report	예술·사회〉미술: 그림의 창작·유통 보존에 관한 이야기 Report

* 똑똑한 영어 읽기 Wise & Wide 시리즈는 60권까지 계속 출간됩니다.

How to Use This Book

●Before Reading

어떤 분야, 어떤 종류의 이야기를 읽게 될지, 줄거리는 어떠한지 미리 쉽게 알아 볼 수 있어요.

●영어 본문

미국, 영국의 우수한 작가들이 집필하여 각 단계의 수준에 맞는 영어 문장·표현의 참맛을 제대로 느낄 수 있어요.

●Pop Quiz

쪽지 시험처럼 핵심을 찌르는 퀴즈로 해당 페이지의 내용을 잘 이해하고 있는 지 바로 확인해 보세요.

●어휘 설명

일일이 사전을 찾아보지 않아도 주요 어휘와 표현의 뜻을 알 수 있어요.

●Aha! 상식

Aha! 표시가 붙어 있는 문장에 대한 설명은 여기서 확인하세요. 문화 상식, 영어 구문이나 문법 상식, 그리고 과학·경제 상식까지! 각 분야의 상식들이 알차게 들어 있어 읽는 재미가 두 배예요.

Before Reading

Things to Know about Paintings
그림에 관해 알아야 할 것들

Level 6-10, Lexile®950L
•예술·사회D미술
•report

그림과 인간

이것은 인류 최초의 그림 작품으로 알려진 스페인의 알타미라 동굴 벽화예요. 잃어버린 개를 찾으러 동굴에 들어간 소녀가 벽 가득히 그려진 수만 년 전 동물 그림들을 발견해서 세상에 알려졌어요. 이 동굴 벽화들은 일반적인 선사시대의 다른 동굴 벽화보다 더 섬세하고 예술적으로 그려진 것으로 유명해요. 이것은 인류가 아주 오래전부터 그림을 그려왔고, 더욱더 아름답고 사실적으로 그리려고 노력했다는 것을 말해줘요. 시간이 흐르고 기술이 발전하면서 사람들은 더 다양한 소재, 더 진보한 그림 기법, 더 좋은 재료들을 이용해서 그림을 그리게 됐어요. 그림을 통하면, 언어가 다르거나 글자를 몰라도 메시지를 주고받을 수 있고, 수백 년 전 살았던 화가의 마음을 읽을 수도 있어요. 뛰어난 그림을 보며 감동하고, 흥미로운 그림을 보며 즐거움을 얻을 수도 있죠. 이렇듯 그림은 인간의 역사에서 큰 부분을 차지하는 중요한 요소랍니다.

줄거리

우리가 하나의 미술 작품을 감상하기 위해서는 어떤 것들이 필요할까요? 일단 작품을 만들어내는 작가가 있어야겠죠! 까마득히 오래전 선사시대의 인류부터 현대의 꼬마 천재 화가까지, 우리는 다양한 인물들이 각기 다른 이유로 미술 작품을 만든다는 사실을 배울 거예요. 작가가 작품을 그리는 것도 단순한 일은 아니에요. 우선 그림을 그리기 전에 무엇을 그릴지, 그리고 어떤 재료를 사용할지를 결정해야 해요. 특히 그림의 주재료인 물감은 종류에 따라 특성이 달라서, 무엇을 선택하는지에 따라 결과물이 크게 달라진답니다. 주제와 재료가 확정되면 본격적인 작업이 시작돼요. 이때 작가는 그림을 그릴 알맞은 작업실이 필요해지죠. 우리는 여러 작가의 작업실을 엿보며 그들의 작업 스타일에 대해 알아볼 거예요. 작품이 완성되면 그것으로 끝일까요? 놀랍게도 우리가 미술 작품을 감상하기 위해서는 작가만이 아니라 다른 여러 직종의 사람들 도움이 필요하답니다. 자, 그럼 작가와 작품, 그리고 작품 완성 이후에 관여하는 사람들까지, 그림에 관한 모든 것들을 살펴 봅시다!

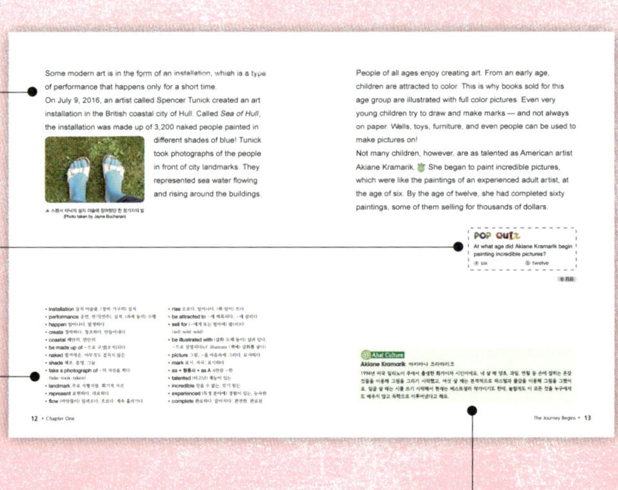

Some modern art is in the form of an installation, which is a type of performance that happens only for a short time. On July 9, 2016, an artist called Spencer Tunick created an art installation in the British coastal city of Hull. Called *Sea of Hull*, the installation was made up of 3,200 naked people painted in different shades of blue! Tunick took photographs of the people in front of city landmarks. They represented sea water flowing and rising around the buildings.

▲ 스펜서 터닉의 설치 미술에 참여했던 한 참가자의 발
(Photo taken by Jayne Buchanan)

People of all ages enjoy creating art. From an early age, children are attracted to color. This is why books sold for this age group are illustrated with full color pictures. Even very young children try to draw and make marks — and not always on paper. Walls, toys, furniture, and even people can be used to make pictures on!
Not many children, however, are as talented as American artist Akiane Kramarik. She began to paint incredible pictures, which were like the paintings of an experienced adult artist, at the age of six. By the age of twelve, she had completed sixty paintings, some of them selling for thousands of dollars.

POP Quiz
At what age did Akiane Kramarik begin painting incredible pictures?
ⓐ six　　ⓑ twelve

- **installation** 설치 미술품, (장비, 가구의) 설치
- **performance** 공연, 연기[연주], 실적, (과제 등의) 수행
- **happen** 일어나다, 발생하다
- **create** 창작하다, 창조하다, 만들어내다
- **coastal** 해안의, 연안의
- **be made up of** ~으로 구성[조직]되다
- **naked** 벌거벗은, 아무것도 걸치지 않은
- **shade** 색조, 음영, 그늘
- **take a photograph of** ~의 사진을 찍다 (take-took-taken)
- **landmark** 주요 지형지물, 획기적 사건
- **represent** 표현하다, 대표하다
- **flow** (바닷물이) 밀려오다, 흐르다, 계속 흘러가다
- **rise** 오르다, 일어나다, (해·달이) 뜨다
- **be attracted to** ~에 매료되다, ~에 끌리다
- **sell for** (~액 또는 얼마에) 팔리자 (sell-sold-sold)
- **be illustrated with** (삽화·도해 등이) 실려 있다, ~으로 설명되다(cf. illustrate (책에) 삽화를 넣다)
- **picture** 그림, ~을 마음속에 그리다, 묘사하다
- **mark** 표시, 자국, 표시하다
- **as + 형용사 + as A** A만큼 ~한
- **talented** (타고난) 재능이 있는
- **incredible** 믿을 수 없는, 믿기 힘든
- **experienced** (특정 분야에) 경험이 있는, 능숙한
- **complete** 완료하다, 끝마치다, 완전한, 완료된

Aha! Culture
Akiane Kramarik 아키아나 크라마리크
1994년 미국 일리노이 주에서 출생한 화가이자 시인이에요. 네 살 때 양초, 과일, 연필 등 손에 잡히는 온갖 것들을 이용해 그림을 그리기 시작했고, 여섯 살 때는 본격적으로 파스텔과 물감을 이용해 그림을 그렸어요. 일곱 살 때는 시를 쓰기 시작해서 현재는 베스트셀러 작가이기도 한데, 놀랍게도 이 모든 것을 누구에게도 배우지 않고 독학으로 이루어냈다고 해요.

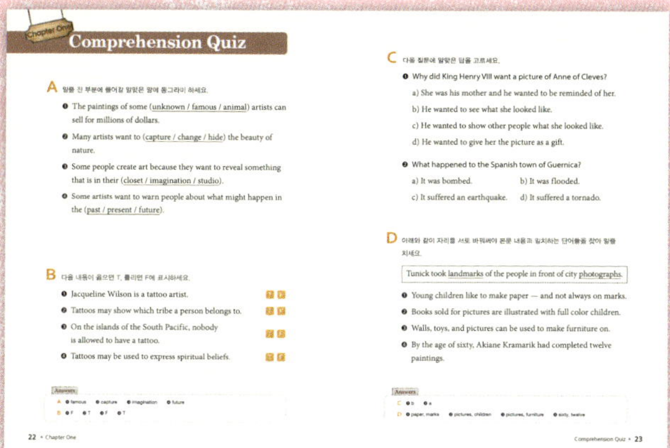

●Comprehension Quiz

한 chapter를 다 읽은 후에는 다양한 문제를 풀어보며 내용을 제대로 이해했는지 정리하고 넘어가세요.

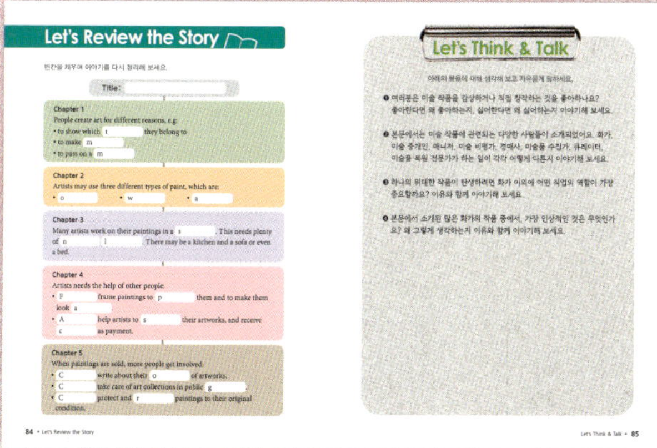

●Let's Review the Story /
●Let's Think & Talk

Organizer의 빈칸을 채우며 전체 이야기를 요약하고, 질문에 답하며 내 생각과 느낌을 자유롭게 정리해 봐요. 훗날 논술에 대비할 논리력과 사고력을 기를 수 있어요.

부록

Audio CD

책의 내용이 그대로 담긴 오디오 CD. 오디오 극장처럼 생생하고 재미있는 음원을 만나보세요. (MP3 파일 PC·모바일 무료 다운로드)

온·오프라인 독후 테스트 & 온라인 단어 퀴즈·단어 리스트

독후 테스트는 책 또는 온라인으로 풀어볼 수 있어요. 온라인으로 풀면 좀 더 자세한 응시 결과와 함께, 전체 응시자들과 비교했을 때 내 실력이 어느 정도 위치인지도 알아볼 수 있어요.

추가로 제공되는 온라인 단어 퀴즈도 풀어보시고, 단어 리스트도 PC나 모바일로 무료로 다운로드 받으세요.

www.darakwon.co.kr

Before Reading

Things to Know about Paintings
그림에 관해 알아야 할 것들

Level 6-10,
Lexile®950L

•예술·사회〉미술
•report

그림과 인간

이것은 인류 최초의 그림 작품으로 알려진 스페인의 알타미라 동굴 벽화예요. 잃어버린 개를 찾으러 동굴에 들어간 소녀가 벽 가득히 그려진 수만 년 전 동물 그림들을 발견해서 세상에 알려졌어요. 이 동굴 벽화들은 일반적인 선사시대의 다른 동굴 벽화보다 더 섬세하고 예술적으로 그려진 것으로 유명해요. 이것은 인류가 아주 오래전부터 그림을 그려왔고, 더욱더 아름답고 사실적으로 그리려고 노력했다는 것을 말해줘요. 시간이 흐르고 기술이 발전하면서 사람들은 더 다양한 소재, 더 진보한 그림 기법, 더 좋은 재료들을 이용해서 그림을 그리게 됐어요. 그림을 통하면, 언어가 다르거나 글자를 몰라도 메시지를 주고받을 수 있고, 수백 년 전 살았던 화가의 마음을 읽을 수도 있어요. 뛰어난 그림을 보며 감동하고, 흥미로운 그림을 보며 즐거움을 얻을 수도 있죠. 이렇듯 그림은 인간의 역사에서 큰 부분을 차지하는 중요한 요소랍니다.

줄거리

우리가 하나의 미술 작품을 감상하기 위해서는 어떤 것들이 필요할까요? 일단 작품을 만들어내는 작가가 있어야겠죠! 까마득히 오래전 선사시대의 인류부터 현대의 꼬마 천재 화가까지, 우리는 다양한 인물들이 각기 다른 이유로 미술 작품을 만든다는 사실을 배울 거예요. 작가가 작품을 그리는 것도 단순한 일은 아니에요. 우선 그림을 그리기 전에 무엇을 그릴지, 그리고 어떤 재료를 사용할지를 결정해야 해요. 특히 그림의 주재료인 물감은 종류에 따라 특성이 달라서, 무엇을 선택하는지에 따라 결과물이 크게 달라진답니다. 주제와 재료가 확정되면 본격적인 작업이 시작돼요. 이때 작가는 그림을 그릴 알맞은 작업실이 필요해지죠. 우리는 여러 작가의 작업실을 엿보며 그들의 작업 스타일에 대해 알아볼 거예요. 작품이 완성되면 그것으로 끝일까요? 놀랍게도 우리가 미술 작품을 감상하기 위해서는 작가만이 아니라 다른 여러 직종의 사람들 도움이 필요하답니다. 자, 그럼 작가와 작품, 그리고 작품 완성 이후에 관여하는 사람들까지, 그림에 관한 모든 것들을 살펴봅시다!

Contents

Things to Know about Paintings

그림에 관해 알아야 할 것들

2　About Wise & Wide
4　How to Use This Book
6　Before Reading

Chapter One
10　The Journey Begins 여행이 시작되다
22　Comprehension Quiz

Chapter Two
24　Getting Ready to Paint 그림 그릴 준비하기
40　Comprehension Quiz

Chapter Three
42　Painting a Picture 그림 그리기
54　Comprehension Quiz

Chapter Four
56　The Finished Painting 완성된 그림
64　Comprehension Quiz

Chapter Five
66　Selling, Restoring, and Viewing 판매, 복원, 그리고 감상
82　Comprehension Quiz

84　Let's Review the Story
85　Let's Think & Talk
86　Let's Review the Story 정답
87　전문 번역
101　독후 테스트

그림에 관해 알아야 할 것들

Things to Know about Paintings

The Journey Begins

여행이 시작되다

What exactly is art? Is it any drawing or painting? Of course not — there are many other forms of art, including sculpture, photography, textiles, and ceramics.

Modern art is displayed at the Tate Modern Gallery in London. Over the years, it has included piles of bricks, giant slides and a hall filled with millions of ceramic sunflower seeds!

▲ 테이트 모던 미술관의 내부

In an episode of the TV series *The Simpsons*, Homer tries — and fails — to make a barbecue out of scrap metal. But it is mistaken for a piece of modern art and displayed for the public to view.

- **journey** (멀리 가는) 여행, 여정
- **exactly** 정확히, 바로, 엄밀히 말해서
- **art** 미술(품), 예술, 기술
- **drawing** (연필·펜 등으로 그린) 그림, 소묘
- **form** 종류, 유형, 형태
- **including** ~을 포함하여, ~을 비롯하여
  (*cf.* include 포함하다, 포함시키다)
- **sculpture** 조각품, 조형물
- **textile** 직물, 섬유
- **ceramic** 도자기, 세라믹
- **modern** 현대의, 근대적인, 오늘날의
- **display** 전시하다, 진열하다, 보여주다
- **over the years** 몇 년간

- **pile** 쌓아 놓은 것, 무더기, 더미
- **slide** 미끄럼틀, 미끄러짐, (환등기·현미경 등) 슬라이드
- **filled with** ~으로 가득 찬
- **seed** 씨, 씨앗, 종자
- **episode** (라디오·텔레비전 연속 프로의) 1회 방송분,
  (사람의 인생·소설 등에서 중요하거나 재미있는) 사건
- **barbecue** 바비큐[숯불구이]용 그릴, 바비큐 파티
- **scrap metal** 고철(*cf.* scrap 조각, 파편, 폐품)
- **mistake for** ~으로 오해하다
  (mistake-mistook-mistaken)
- **the public** 대중, 일반 사람들
- **view** (세심히 살피며) 보다, (텔레비전·영화 등을) 보다;
  경관, 견해

Aha! Culture

The Simpsons 심슨 가족

미국 폭스(Fox) 방송사의 대표적인 애니메이션 시트콤 프로그램이에요. 1989년에 첫 방송이 이루어진 이후 현재까지 총 28개의 시즌이 방송된, 미국 역사상 최장수 프로그램 중 하나랍니다. 아빠인 호머 심슨, 엄마 마지 심슨과 바트, 리사, 매기라는 이름의 자녀들로 구성된 미국 중산층 가정의 일상이 주로 다루어지는데 미국의 문화와 사회를 풍자하는 내용으로 많은 사람에게 사랑받고 있어요.

Some modern art is in the form of an installation, which is a type of performance that happens only for a short time.

On July 9, 2016, an artist called Spencer Tunick created an art installation in the British coastal city of Hull. Called *Sea of Hull*, the installation was made up of 3,200 naked people painted in

▲ 스펜서 터닉의 설치 미술에 참여했던 한 참가자의 발
(Photo taken by Jayne Buchanan)

different shades of blue! Tunick took photographs of the people in front of city landmarks. They represented sea water flowing and rising around the buildings.

- **installation** 설치 미술품, (장비·가구의) 설치
- **performance** 공연, 연기[연주], 실적, (과제 등의) 수행
- **happen** 일어나다, 발생하다
- **create** 창작하다, 창조하다, 만들어내다
- **coastal** 해안의, 연안의
- **be made up of** ~으로 구성[조직]되다
- **naked** 벌거벗은, 아무것도 걸치지 않은
- **shade** 색조, 음영, 그늘
- **take a photograph of** ~의 사진을 찍다
  (take-took-taken)
- **landmark** 주요 지형지물, 획기적 사건
- **represent** 표현하다, 대표하다
- **flow** (바닷물이) 밀려오다, 흐르다, 계속 흘러가다

- **rise** 오르다, 일어나다, (해·달이) 뜨다
- **be attracted to** ~에 매혹되다, ~에 끌리다
- **sell for** (~에게 또는 얼마에) 팔(리)다
  (sell-sold-sold)
- **be illustrated with** (삽화·도해 등이) 실려 있다,
  ~으로 설명되다(*cf.* illustrate (책에) 삽화를 넣다)
- **picture** 그림; ~을 마음속에 그리다, 묘사하다
- **mark** 표시, 자국; 표시하다
- **as + 형용사 + as A** A만큼 ~한
- **talented** (타고난) 재능이 있는
- **incredible** 믿을 수 없는, 믿기 힘든
- **experienced** (특정 분야에) 경험이 있는, 능숙한
- **complete** 완료하다, 끝마치다; 완전한, 완료된

People of all ages enjoy creating art. From an early age, children are attracted to color. This is why books sold for this age group are illustrated with full color pictures. Even very young children try to draw and make marks — and not always on paper. Walls, toys, furniture, and even people can be used to make pictures on!

Not many children, however, are as talented as American artist Akiane Kramarik.  She began to paint incredible pictures, which were like the paintings of an experienced adult artist, at the age of six. By the age of twelve, she had completed sixty paintings, some of them selling for thousands of dollars.

POP QUIZ

At what age did Akiane Kramarik begin painting incredible pictures?

ⓐ six   ⓑ twelve

ⓔ 吕요

🌐 Aha! Culture

Akiane Kramarik 아키아나 크라마리크

1994년 미국 일리노이 주에서 출생한 화가이자 시인이에요. 네 살 때 양초, 과일, 연필 등 손에 잡히는 온갖 것들을 이용해 그림을 그리기 시작했고, 여섯 살 때는 본격적으로 파스텔과 물감을 이용해 그림을 그렸어요. 일곱 살 때는 시를 쓰기 시작해서 현재는 베스트셀러 작가이기도 한데, 놀랍게도 이 모든 것을 누구에게도 배우지 않고 독학으로 이루어냈다고 해요.

▲ 새틴바우어새

▲ 새틴바우어새가 둥지에 모아놓은 파란색 물건들

Some people believe that even animals create works of art. In Australia, male satin bowerbirds collect blue items and arrange them in structures called "bowers" to attract females. Flowers, pieces of glass, drinking straws, and clothespins have all been found in their carefully built bowers.

The keepers at the St. Louis Zoo in the U.S.A. allow some of their animals to experiment with paints. Snakes, apes, penguins and even insects can make paint marks on canvases. Their artworks are sold to raise money for zoo projects.

- **satin bowerbird** 새틴바우어새
- **item** 물품, 항목
- **arrange** 배치하다, 준비하다, 정리하다
- **structure** 구조, 건축물
- **bower** 그늘진 휴게소(정자), 나무 그늘
- **clothespin** 빨래집게
- **keeper** (동물원의) 사육사, 책임자, 관리자
- **allow** 허용하다, ~할 수 있게 하다
- **experiment with** ~으로 실험하다, ~을 실험하다
- **ape** 유인원, 원숭이
- **insect** 곤충, 벌레
- **artwork** 미술품, 삽화, 공예품
- **raise money** 돈을 마련하다

- **project** (대규모) 계획 사업, 기획, 연구 과제
- **date from** ~부터 시작되다
- **prehistoric times** 선사시대
- **up to** ~까지
- **continent** 대륙, 육지
- **tool** 도구, 수단
- **pigment** 안료, 색소
- **earth** 흙, 지구, 땅
- **yellowish** 노르스름한, 누르스름한
- **probably** 아마, 십중팔구는(= perhaps)
- **pass on** ~을 물려주다, ~을 전하다
  (*cf*. pass 건네주다, 지나가다)
- **nearby** 가까이; 가까운

People of all cultures create art, and it is an important way to learn about history. Cave paintings date from prehistoric times, up to 40,000 years ago.

▲ 선사시대의 동굴 벽화

They can be found on most continents.

They were painted on cave walls using fingers or simple tools.

Colors — or pigments — were made using earth and rocks.

This is why most cave paintings are red, black, brown, or yellowish colors.

In the 2013 movie, *The Croods*, a caveman makes pictures on the wall of a cave to tell the story of his family. They were probably also a way of passing on information about which animals lived nearby and how to catch them.

This is why most cave paintings are red, black, brown, or yellowish colors. 그렇기 때문에 대부분의 동굴 벽화들은 빨간색, 검은색, 갈색, 또는 누르스름한 색이다.

앞에서 언급한 어떤 사실에 대해 그 이유를 설명할 때 사용하는 표현인 this is why ~는 '그렇기 때문에 (= 그래서) ~'의 뜻이에요.

ex. The scenery here is wonderful. This is why I live here. 여기 경치는 굉장하다. 그래서 내가 여기서 사는 것이다.

In some cultures, people create art on their own bodies in the form of tattoos. You can read about a woman who did this in Jacqueline Wilson's novel for children, *The Illustrated Mum*.

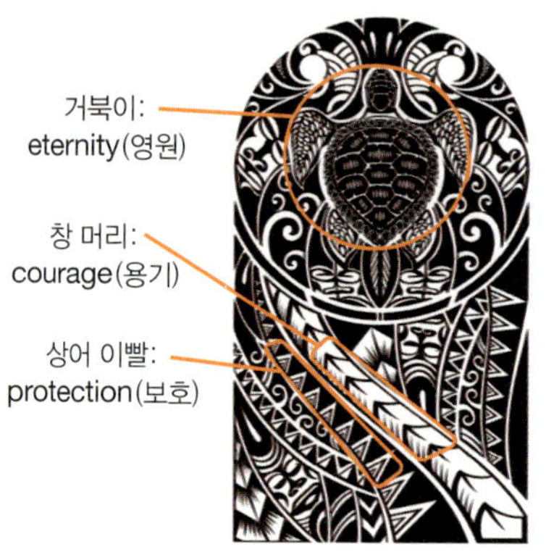

▲ 문신 속 다양한 상징들과
그 속에 담긴 의미들

Often, people do it because they like the way it looks. But in some cultures, such as those of the island nations in the South Pacific, these tattooed symbols have important meanings. They may show which family or tribe a person belongs to. They may be used to express religious or spiritual beliefs.

- **own** 자기 자신의, 독자적인; 소유하다(= possess)
- **tattoo** 문신; 문신을 새기다
- **mum** 엄마, mom의 영국식 표기
- **look** ~해 보이다, ~한 것 같다, 보다
- **such as** ~와 같은, 예를 들어
- **tribe** 부족, 종족
- **belong to** ~에 속하다, ~의 것이다
- **express** (감정·의견 등을) 표현하다, 나타내다
- **religious** 종교의, 신앙심이 깊은
- **spiritual** 정신의, 정신적인
- **belief** (복수) 종교적 믿음, 신념, 확신

Aha! Culture

Polynesian tattoo 폴리네시아 지역의 문신

남태평양에는 수많은 섬이 넓은 지역에 분포되어 있는데, 이 지역의 섬들을 한데 묶어 '폴리네시아'라고 불러요. 뉴질랜드, 하와이, 사모아, 이스터 섬 등이 여기에 해당하죠. 이 지역 사람들은 전통적으로 온몸에 많은 문신을 했어요. 이들은 다양한 의미를 가진 무늬를 몸에 새겨넣음으로써 건강과 장수를 기원하고 가문과 부족의 전통을 기리며, 위험으로부터 몸을 지키고자 했죠. 영어의 *tattoo*라는 단어 자체도 '기록하다'라는 뜻의 폴리네시아어 *tatau*에서 기원했답니다.

Why else do people create art? Some people do it to make money, like any other job. Before photographs existed, artists painted portraits of people to show what they looked like.

When King Henry VIII was on the throne of England in 1539, he sent the painter Hans Holbein to Germany. Holbein's task was to paint a picture of a young woman called Anne of Cleves. Henry was thinking of marrying her, and he wanted to see what she looked like. This was the only way of showing Henry what she looked like.

▲ 한스 홀바인이 그린 영국의 왕 헨리8세의 초상화

Who painted a portrait of Anne of Cleves?
ⓐ Anne of Cleves
ⓑ Hans Holbein

ⓑ 답정

- **else** (그 밖의) 다른
- **make money** (많은) 돈을 벌다, 부자가 되다
- **exist** 존재하다, 살다
- **portrait** 초상화, 인물화
- **look like** ~인 것처럼 보이다, ~할 것 같다
- **be on the throne of** ~의 왕위에 있다
- **task** 과제, 업무, (힘든) 일
- **Cleves** 클레베(독일 서부의 도시)
- **marry** ~와 결혼하다

Holbein produced a pleasant portrait, so Henry agreed to marry her. But when he saw Anne in real life, he said that she looked like a fat horse! Not surprisingly, Holbein was never again asked to produce paintings for the king.

In modern times, photographers take pictures of people, families, and even pets to make money.

The paintings of some famous artists can sell for millions of dollars, although sadly many artists do not become famous until after they are dead.

- **produce** (특히 필요한 기술을 들여) 만들어내다, (상품을 대량으로) 생산하다, (연극·영화 등을) 제작하다
- **pleasant** 호감이 가는, 기분 좋은, 쾌적한
- **in real life** 실제로, 실생활에서
- **not surprisingly** 당연히, 놀랍지 않게
- **although** 비록 ~이긴 하지만, 그러나
- **sadly** 안타깝게도, 슬프게, 유감스럽게도

Aha! English

~ although sadly many artists do not become famous until after they are dead.

~ 하지만, 안타깝게도 많은 작가가 세상을 떠난 후에야 비로소 유명해진다.

not A until B는 'B하고 나서야 비로소 A하다(= B할 때까지는 A하지 않다)'의 뜻이에요.

ex. I didn't realize the fact until I became much older. 나는 나이를 훨씬 더 먹고 나서야 비로소 그 사실을 깨달았다.

Many people create art simply because they enjoy it, or because they want to learn something new. They can develop skills and understanding. Perhaps they want to capture the beauty of nature or to try and reveal something that is in their imagination. Perhaps they want to express an emotion such as joy, anger, or sadness.

- **simply** 그냥, 그저, 그야말로, 정말로
- **develop** 발달시키다, 발달하다, 개발하다
- **skill** 기량, 기술
- **understanding** (특정 주제·상황에 대한) 이해, (암묵적인) 합의
- **capture** (사진이나 글로 감정·분위기 등을) 정확히 포착하다, 포로로 잡다, 점유하다, (관심·상상력 등을) 사로잡다
- **try and + 동사원형** ~하려 노력하다, 애쓰다(= try to + 동사원형)
- **reveal** 드러내다, 폭로하다
- **imagination** 상상, 상상력, 창의력
- **emotion** 감정, 정서

Other people create art because they want to pass on a message. They want to tell a story of something that has happened, or they want to warn people about something that might happen in the future.

For example, Pablo Picasso's famous painting, *Guernica*, was painted after a Spanish town called Guernica was bombed. It records the suffering of the people in that village. It also gives a message to everyone that war is a bad thing.

▲ 스페인 내전 당시 몇 차례의 폭격을 받은 이후의 게르니카 마을

- **warn** 경고하다, 강력히 충고하다
- **bomb** 폭격하다; 폭탄
- **record** 기록하다, 녹화하다; 기록, 음반
- **suffering** (정신적·육체적) 고통, 괴로움

Aha! Culture

Guernica & Spanish Civil War 게르니카 마을과 스페인 내전

1936년, 선거를 통해 새로운 스페인 정부가 들어서고 반년도 지나지 않아 프란시스코 프랑코라는 한 장군이 반란을 일으켜요. 결국 스페인은 정부군과 프랑코 장군이 이끄는 반란군들로 나뉘어 전쟁을 치르게 돼요. 이때 히틀러가 이끄는 독일의 나치 정권은 프랑코 장군의 반란군을 지원하기 위해 수만 명의 군대를 파병했고, 이들에 의해 스페인의 많은 지역이 크게 피해를 보고 말았어요. 게르니카 마을이 바로 그중 하나였죠. 스페인 내전은 결국 수많은 민간인 피해자들을 만든 뒤 프랑코 장군과 반란군의 승리로 끝났어요.

Art is a way of sharing deep thoughts and emotions in such a way that people who view the art can also experience them. It is a way of bringing people together and making them realize that they are not alone.

So art is basically about communication from one person to another. Let us imagine an artist who has an emotion or a message that he or she wants to share. Let us also picture a viewer who sees the artwork and receives the message. How does the message get passed from one to the other? What other people are involved in passing it on? Let us investigate the journey that paintings take, from beginning to end.

- **share** 공유하다, 나누다
- **in such a way that** ~와 같은 방식으로
- **bring together** ~을 합치다, ~을 긁어모으다
  (bring-brought-brought)
- **realize** 깨닫다, 실현하다

- **basically** 근본적으로, 기본적으로
- **communication** 의사소통, 연락, 통신 (수단들)
- **receive** 받다, 받아들이다
- **be involved in** ~에 개입[관계]되다, ~에 몰두하다
- **investigate** 수사하다, 조사하다

Comprehension Quiz

A 밑줄 친 부분에 들어갈 알맞은 말에 동그라미 하세요.

❶ The paintings of some (unknown / famous / animal) artists can sell for millions of dollars.

❷ Many artists want to (capture / change / hide) the beauty of nature.

❸ Some people create art because they want to reveal something that is in their (closet / imagination / studio).

❹ Some artists want to warn people about what might happen in the (past / present / future).

B 다음 내용이 옳으면 T, 틀리면 F에 표시하세요.

❶ Jacqueline Wilson is a tattoo artist.　　T　F

❷ Tattoos may show which tribe a person belongs to.　　T　F

❸ On the islands of the South Pacific, nobody is allowed to have a tattoo.　　T　F

❹ Tattoos may be used to express spiritual beliefs.　　T　F

Answers

A　❶ famous　❷ capture　❸ imagination　❹ future

B　❶ F　❷ T　❸ F　❹ T

C 다음 질문에 알맞은 답을 고르세요.

❶ Why did King Henry VIII want a picture of Anne of Cleves?

a) She was his mother and he wanted to be reminded of her.

b) He wanted to see what she looked like.

c) He wanted to show other people what she looked like.

d) He wanted to give her the picture as a gift.

❷ What happened to the Spanish town of Guernica?

a) It was bombed.   b) It was flooded.

c) It suffered an earthquake.   d) It suffered a tornado.

D 아래와 같이 자리를 서로 바꿔써야 본문 내용과 일치하는 단어들을 찾아 밑줄 치세요.

> Tunick took <u>landmarks</u> of the people in front of city <u>photographs</u>.

❶ Young children like to make paper — and not always on marks.

❷ Books sold for pictures are illustrated with full color children.

❸ Walls, toys, and pictures can be used to make furniture on.

❹ By the age of sixty, Akiane Kramarik had completed twelve paintings.

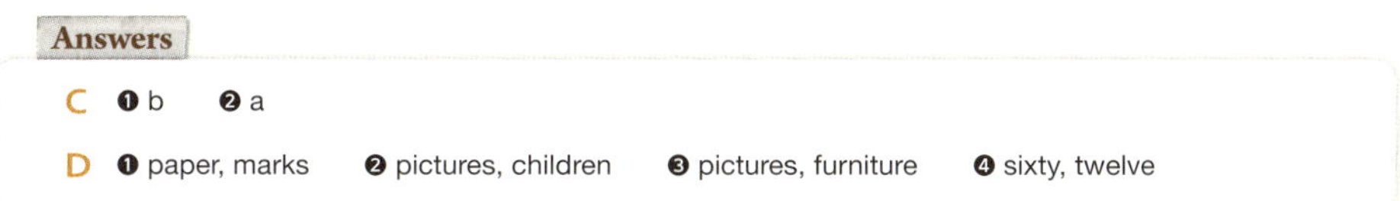

Answers

C   **❶** b   **❷** a

D   **❶** paper, marks   **❷** pictures, children   **❸** pictures, furniture   **❹** sixty, twelve

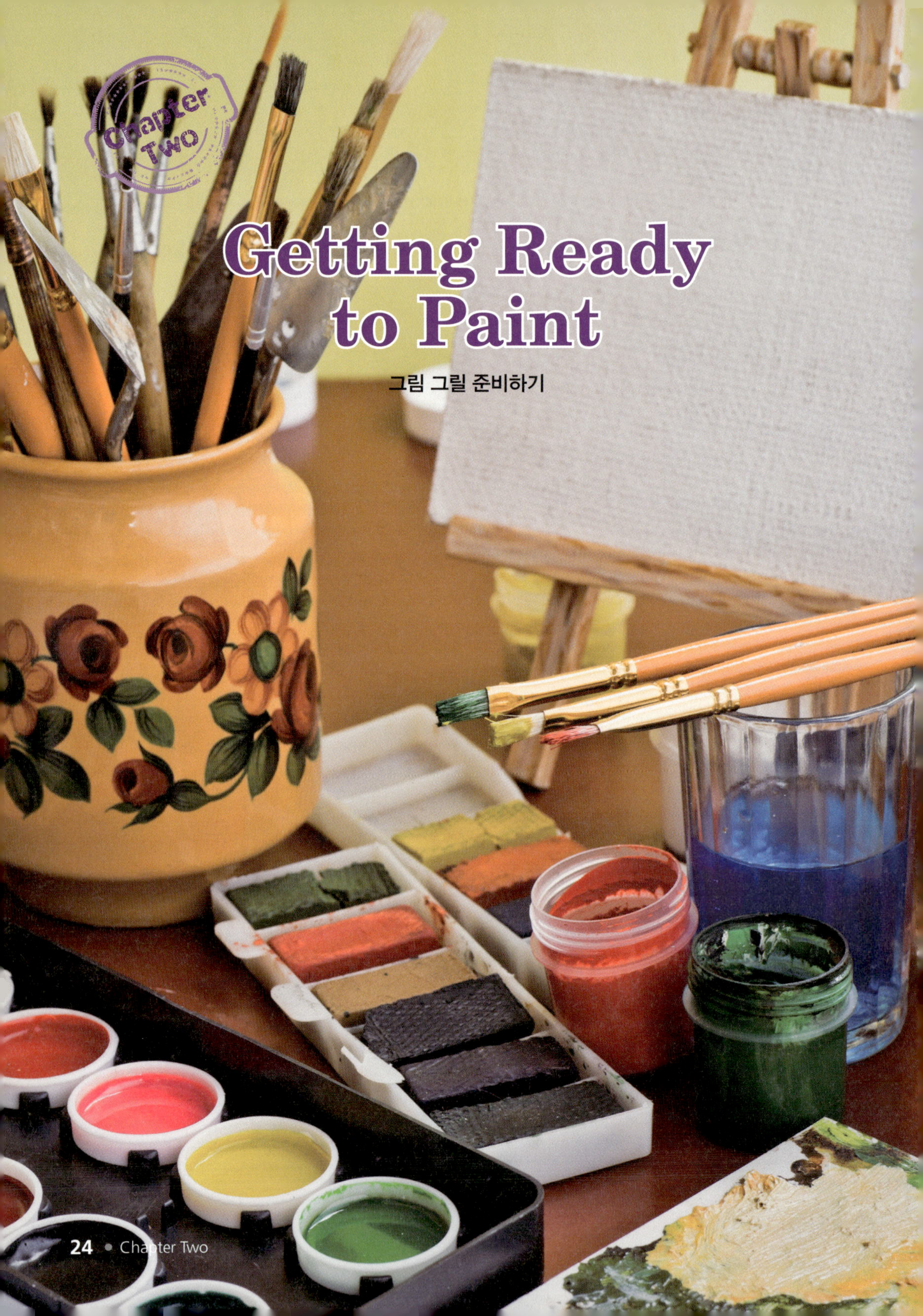

Chapter Two

Getting Ready
to Paint

그림 그릴 준비하기

How does an artist decide what to paint? Artists get their inspiration from all kinds of different places. Most would agree that ideas can come from anywhere, and when they are least expected!

Some artists paint real objects, which may be natural or made by humans. This is called a "still life" painting.  The artist seeks to capture a realistic image of something that will not last.

POP QUIZ

What is painted in a "still life" painting?

ⓐ real objects
ⓑ people

ⓔ 吕&

- **get ready** 준비를 하다(get-got-gotten)
- **decide** 결정하다, 결심하다
- **inspiration** (특히 예술적 창조를 가능하게 하는) 영감
- **come from** ~에서 나오다(*cf.* come 오다, (물품·상품이) 나오다, 생산되다, 제공되다)
- **least** 가장 적게, 최소로; 가장 적은, 최소의
- **expect** 예상하다, 기대하다, 기다리다

- **object** 물건, (욕망·연구·관심의) 대상, 목표
- **natural** 자연의, 천연의
- **still life** 정물화, 정물화 기법
- **seek to + 동사원형** ~하려고 시도하다 (seek-sought-sought)
- **realistic** 사실적인, 실제 그대로의, 현실을 직시하는
- **last** 지속되다, (특정 시간 동안) 계속되다, 버티다

🌐 Aha! Culture

still life painting 정물화

정물화란 우리 주변에 있는 생명이 없으며 움직이지 못하는 물건, 즉 꽃이나 식물, 과일, 악기, 식기, 책 등을 그린 회화를 통칭하는 말이에요. 정물화는 고대 로마의 모자이크나 벽화에서도 발견될 정도로 역사가 오래됐는데, 중세시대에는 인물화에 치중해 많이 그려지지 않았어요. 정물화가 독립된 그림의 종류로 확립된 것은 17세기 이후로 특히 네덜란드에서 발달했는데, 브뤼헐, 루벤스, 그리고 렘브란트 같은 화가들이 많이 그렸어요.

This is why flowers and fruit were popular choices for still life paintings in the past, before photography was popular, and are still popular choices today. Other artists choose more unusual subjects, such as this painting called *Mound of Butter*. It was painted by French artist Antoine Vallon in the 19th century. Many artists are inspired by nature, whether they choose to paint individual animals or plants or whether they choose to paint landscapes.

Botanical artist Martin J. Allen paints highly detailed paintings of plants. He is inspired by the moment when a flower bud begins to open. This idea of capturing the moment of change inspired a whole collection of paintings exhibited in 1987.

▲ Antoine Vallon(앙트안느 발롱)의
Mound of Butter(버터 더미)

▲ 1800년대의 식물화가 Charles Antoine
(샤를 앙트안느)의 작품

Some artists are inspired by their dreams. A French artist called Odilon Redon painted what he called "black" pictures, which were made up of images which were in his dreams and nightmares. 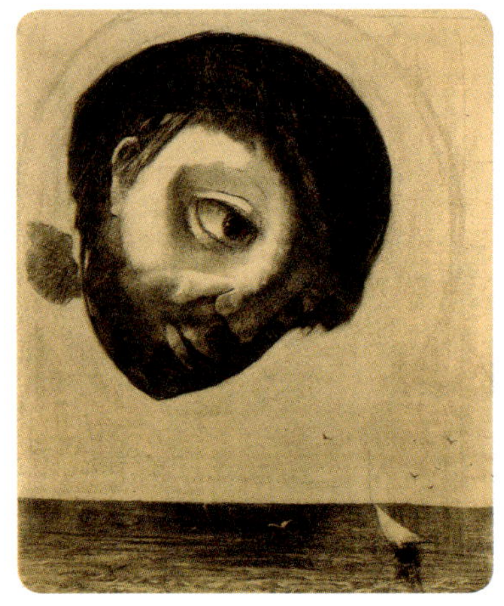
In 1878, he painted *Guardian Spirit of the Waters*, which contains a face hovering over the sea.

▲ Odilon Redon(오딜롱 르동)의
Guardian Spirit of the Waters(물의 수호 정령)

- **choice** 선택, 선택권
- **past** 과거; 과거의; 지나서
- **subject** (논의 등의) 주제[대상], 문제, 학과
- **mound** 더미, 무더기, 흙더미
- **be inspired by** ~에 의해 영감을 받다
  (*cf.* inspire 영감을 주다)
- **whether** ~이든 아니든, ~인지 아닌지
- **individual** 각각의, 개인의; 개인
- **landscape** 풍경, 풍경화
- **botanical** 식물의, 식물로 만들어진, 식물학의
- **highly** 매우, 높이, 고도로
- **detailed** 상세한, 세부적인

- **bud** 꽃봉오리, 싹
- **whole** 전체의, 모든, 온전한
- **collection** 컬렉션(신작품 발표회), 수집품, 무리, 수집, 모음집
- **exhibit** 전시하다, (감정·특질 등을) 드러내다
- **be made up of** ~으로 구성되다
- **nightmare** 악몽, 아주 끔찍한 일
- **guardian spirit** (토지·인간 등의) 수호신, 신령
- **contain** 들어 있다, 포함하다, 함유하다
- **face** 얼굴; 향하다, 마주 보다, 직면하다
- **hover** 맴돌다, 떠다니다

Aha! Culture

Odilon Redon 오딜롱 르동(1840~1916)

프랑스 출신의 인상파 화가예요. 르동은 어린 시절 부모님의 사이가 좋지 않고 건강이 나빴던 탓에 외삼촌의 농장에서 자랐어요. 부모님이 잘 찾아오지 않자 르동은 자신이 버려졌다고 느끼게 되었고, 이런 성장기의 기억은 르동에게 '검고 어두운, 침묵의 시간'으로 남게 되죠. 르동이 훗날 목탄과 석판화 기법을 이용해서 무채색 위주의 '검은' 그림들을 그리게 된 데엔 이런 개인적 경험의 영향도 컸다고 해요.

▲ Vasily Kandinsky(바실리 칸딘스키)의 추상화

Other artists, especially those who paint abstract art (patterns, shapes, and lines with no obvious picture), claim that they get their ideas as they go along. They begin with a feeling, a desire to use a particular color, and then they see how it develops. There is really no limit to where ideas may come from. But once the artist has a strong desire to create, the journey may begin.

Aha! English

But once the artist has a strong desire to create, the journey may begin. 그렇지만 일단 그 화가가 강렬한 창작 욕구를 가지면, 그 여정이 시작될 수 있다.

once가 접속사로 쓰이면 '일단 ~하면'의 뜻이에요. 뒤에는 '주어 + 동사'가 따라와요.

ex. Once you get there, you'll like it. 일단 네가 거기 도착하면, 그곳이 마음에 들 것이다.

Once an artist has decided what image he or she wants to create, the next decisions are the choices of media. An artist must choose what to draw or paint on and what to draw or paint with.

An artist can paint on almost anything. Stone, bark, wood, ceramics, glass, concrete, leather or even the human body are some alternative choices of media. Each of these materials has different properties that may affect how easy or difficult it is to apply paint. They also affect how long the paint will keep its color and appearance.

The artist chooses the medium depending on how the finished piece will look, or what message will be given. For example, an artist may choose to paint on a stone so that people can pick it up and hold it. The way the rock *feels* may be as important as the way it *looks*.

- **especially** 특히, 특별히
- **abstract** 추상적인, 관념적인
- **obvious** 분명한, 확실한
- **claim** 주장하다, 요청하다
- **go along** (활동을) 계속하다, (일 등을) 진척시키다 (go-went-gone)
- **desire** 욕구, 갈망; 바라다
- **particular** 특정한, 특별한
- **limit** 한계, 제한
- **medium** (화가·작가·음악가의) 표현 수단, 매체, 수단, 도구(복수형. media); (치수·양·길이·온도 등이) 중간의
- **bark** 나무껍질, (개 등이) 짖는 소리; (개가) 짖다
- **leather** (무두질을 거친) 가죽
- **alternative** 대체 가능한, 대안이 되는; 대안, 선택이 가능한 것
- **material** 재료, 성분, 소재
- **property** 특성, 재산, 부동산
- **affect** 영향을 미치다, 작용하다
- **apply** (페인트·약 등을) 바르다, 적용하다, 지원하다
- **keep** 유지하다, 지키다, 계속 가지고 있다, 보관하다 (keep-kept-kept)
- **appearance** 겉모습, 외모, 출현
- **depending on** ~에 따라(cf. depend on ~에 달려 있다)
- **pick up** 집다, 태워주다
- **hold** 쥐다, 잡다(hold-held-held)

PASEO DE
LA VIDA

A mural is a picture that is painted directly onto the wall of a building, either inside or outside. Murals can be used to brighten up inner city areas or bare walls. Some street artists paint directly onto sidewalks so that the public can view their work as soon as it is created. There is a particular type of mural or street art called a "trompe l'oeil."  This is French for "mistake of the eye." This is an artwork that forms an illusion or trick. There appears to be a hole in the wall or sidewalk and the viewer sees something completely different beyond.

POP QUIZ

What language are the words "trompe l'oeil" written in?

ⓐ Spanish   ⓑ French

ⓑ 답정

- **mural** 벽화; 벽(면)의
- **directly** (특정한 위치) 바로 ~에, 곧장
- **either A or B** A이든 B이든
- **brighten up** 밝히다, 밝아지다, 환해지다
- **inner city** (빈민가로 변한) 대도시의 중심부, 도심
- **bare** 벌거벗은, 헐벗은, 텅 빈
- **sidewalk** 보도, 인도
- **as soon as** ~하자마자

- **trompe l'oeil** 트롱프뢰유(눈속임 그림)
- **mistake** 실수, 오류
- **illusion** (특히 사람·상황에 대한) 오해, 착각, 환상
- **trick** 속임수, 장난
- **appear** ~인 것 같다, 나타나다
- **completely** 완전히, 전적으로
- **beyond** 건너편에, 그 너머에

🌐 Aha! Culture

trompe l'oeil 트롱프뢰유

'눈을 속이는 그림'이라는 뜻으로, 그림인지 실제 사물인지 모를 정도로 정교하고 사실적으로 묘사된 그림들을 지칭하는 말이에요. 사실은 매우 좁은 공간인데 마치 공간이 더 있는 것처럼 그려서 공간을 넓어 보이게 한다거나, 꽉 막힌 벽이지만 창문과 아름다운 정원을 사실적으로 그려서 창밖에 자연이 펼쳐져 있는 것처럼 보이게 하는 벽화가 트롱프뢰유의 일종이에요.

Graffiti can be a form of art, especially when it is created by world-famous graffiti artist Banksy, who is from England but works all over the world. Nobody knows Banksy's identity, but his works are well known.

▲ Banksy(뱅크시)의 그라피티 작품

There are many Banksy artworks on walls and buildings in London. Many of them are covered in a transparent plastic called Perspex to protect them. But after a while, some of them are painted over, or the wall on which they are painted is removed. Graffiti art rarely lasts a long time, but you can buy photographs or copies of the paintings to keep.

Many artists choose to paint on a flat surface, which can later be hung on a wall for viewing. In the past, artists mainly used wood for this. Leonardo da Vinci's famous *Mona Lisa*, painted in 1503, was painted on poplar wood. Modern artists usually choose either paper or canvas. The choice now depends also on what the artist wants to paint with. There are different types of paint and they require different types of surfaces.

▲ Leonardo da Vinci(레오나르도 다 빈치)의
Mona Lisa(모나리자)

- **graffiti** (보통 공공장소에 하는 불법적) 낙서, 벽화, 그라피티
- **identity** 신분, 정체, 유사성
- **be covered in** ~으로 덮이다
- **transparent** 투명한, 속이 빤히 들여다보이는
- **Perspex** 퍼스펙스(흔히 유리 대용으로 쓰이는 투명 아크릴 수지)
- **protect** 보호하다, 지키다
- **after a while** 잠시 후에, 얼마 후에
- **remove** 제거하다, 치우다, 벗다

- **rarely** 좀처럼[거의] ~ 않는, 드물게
- **copy** 복사본, (책·신문 등의) 한 부; 모사하다, 복사하다
- **flat** 평평한, 납작한, 바람이 빠진
- **surface** 표면, 지면
- **hang** 걸다, 걸리다, 늘어지다(hang-hung-hung)
- **mainly** 주로, 대부분, 대개
- **poplar** 포플러 (나무)
- **require** 필요로 하다, (법·규칙 등에 따라) 요구하다

The three main types of paint are oil, watercolor, and acrylic. Oil paints are stored in tubes and are usually painted onto a surface made of canvas. This is a tough, tightly-woven fabric used for sails and tents as well as for paintings. It is difficult to tear.

Watercolor paints are hard blocks of color that are often stored in a tin. Alternatively, they may be purchased in a tube, squeezed out onto a palette and left to harden. They are usually painted onto paper. To use them the artist adds a little water with a paintbrush to wet the surface of the hard paint. This gives a strong, bright color, when painted onto paper. The more water is added, the thinner the paint will be, so the artist can create a thin, almost transparent "wash."

ⓑ 답정

- **oil** 유화 물감, 기름, 식용유; 기름을 치다
- **watercolor** 수채화 그림물감, 수채화; 수채화로 그려진
- **acrylic** 아크릴 물감; 아크릴로 만든
- **store** 저장하다, 보관하다
- **tough** 질긴, 강인한, 단단한, 힘든
- **tightly-woven** 촘촘히 짜인(cf. weave (직물을) 짜다 (weave-wove-woven))
- **fabric** 직물, 천, (사회·조직 등의) 구조
- **sail** 돛, 항해; 항해하다, 출항하다
- **A as well as B** B뿐만 아니라 A도
- **tear** 찢다, 찢어지다(tear-tore-torn)
- **block** 단단한 사각형 덩어리, (건물) 단지, 구역
- **tin** 주석, (식품 저장용) 통
- **alternatively** 그렇지 않으면, 그 대신에
- **purchase** 구입하다; 구입, 구매한 것
- **squeeze** (특히 손가락으로 꼭) 짜다, (억지로) 비집고 들어가다
- **leave** (어떤 상태·장소 등에) 그대로 두다, 떠나다, (어떤 결과를) 남기다, (관리·처리 등을) 맡기다(leave-left-left)
- **harden** 굳다, 굳히다
- **thin** 옅은, (액체가) 묽은, 얇은, 마른
- **wash** (어떤 표면에 발린 페인트 등 액체의) 얇은 막[겹], 씻기, 세탁; 씻다

▲ 캔버스 위에 그려진 유화

▲ 종이 위에 그려진 수채화

▲ William Berryman(윌리엄 베리먼)의 *Jamaica Hut*(자메이카 오두막)

This watercolor painting by William Berryman, created in the early 1800s, shows the way in which he first sketched the picture and then began to fill it in with watercolor paints. It was painted in Jamaica and has the simple title, *Jamaica Hut.* But the painting was never finished, so perhaps Berryman might have given it a different title when it was complete. What would you call it if it was your painting?

- **fill in** ~을 채우다, 서식을 작성하다
- **hut** 오두막, 막사
- **option** 선택(할 수 있는 것), 선택권
- **century** 세기, 백 년
- **straight** 곧장, 똑바로
- **thick** (액체가) 걸쭉한, 두꺼운, 굵은

- **sticky** 끈적거리는, 달라붙는
- **nail polish** 매니큐어
- **remover** 제거제
- **make a mess** 어지럽히다, 망쳐놓다
  (*cf.* mess 엉망인 상태 / messy 엉망인, 지저분한)

As well as oil and watercolor paints, there is a third option that the modern artist may choose: acrylic paints.  Acrylic paints were invented in the 20th century. They can be used in many different ways, on many different surfaces. Acrylic paints may be mixed with water to make them thinner, like watercolors, or they can be used straight from the tube in their thick, sticky form. Acrylic paints are easy to clean up if they are still wet, because they wash out of clothing or from skin using water. If the paint has dried, it is more difficult, but it can be removed with nail polish remover. Oil paints are much more difficult to remove. So acrylics are good for people who make a mess while they are painting!

🌐 Aha! Culture

acrylic paints 아크릴 물감

아크릴 물감은 맨 처음 벽화를 그리기 위한 용도로 개발되었어요. 온도와 습도의 변화에 항상 노출되어 있는 벽화를 오래 유지하기 위해 개발되었기 때문에 물감의 발색력과 내구도가 매우 뛰어나죠. 또, 착색력이 뛰어나서 종이뿐만 아니라 돌이나 나무, 가죽, 석고와 같이 다양한 표면에 그림을 그릴 수 있어요. 마르는 속도가 무척 빨라 여러 번 겹쳐 그리기에 좋은데, 다만 한번 말라버리면 수정하기가 힘들어요.

▲ Vincent van Gogh(빈센트 반 고흐)의 자화상

▲ 팔레트 나이프를 사용하는 모습

Oil paints and acrylics are good for creating a picture with a rough texture. This is done by putting on thick strokes of paint, either with a brush or a flat knife called a palette knife. This can be clearly seen in Vincent van Gogh's oil painting, *The Starry Night*, painted in 1889.  The rough texture of the paint makes it look as though the stars are moving and shining.

POP QUIZ

Who painted *The Starry Night*?

ⓐ Vincent van Gogh

ⓑ William Berryman

ⓔ 답장

Vincent van Gogh 빈센트 반 고흐

네덜란드 출신의 인상파 화가로, 서양 미술사에서 가장 위대한 화가 중 한 명으로 꼽혀요. 고흐는 20대 후반에야 화가가 되기로 결심하고 작품을 그리기 시작했어요. 그는 서른일곱 살이라는 젊은 나이에 권총 자살로 삶을 마감했는데, 겨우 십 년 남짓한 기간 동안 무려 900여 점의 작품을 그려낸 세계적인 화가가 되었답니다. 다만 그는 살아 있었을 때는 무명이었고 늘 경제적 어려움을 겪었어요. 죽은 뒤 유명해진 대표적인 화가입니다.

▲ Vincent van Gogh의 *The Starry Night*(별이 빛나는 밤)

- **rough** 거친, 껄껄한
- **texture** (직물의) 감촉, 질감
- **put on** ~을 바르다, ~을 입다(put-put-put)
- **stroke** (글씨나 그림의) 획, 타격, (시계나 종이) 치는 소리

- **palette knife** 팔레트 나이프(그림물감 배합이나 요리를 위해 쓰는, 끝이 둥글고 잘 휘어지는 칼)
- **starry** 별이 많은, 별 같은

 **Aha! English**

The rough texture of the paint makes it look <u>as though</u> the stars are moving and shining. 물감의 거칠거칠한 질감은 <u>마치</u> 별들이 움직이고, 빛나고 있는 <u>것처럼</u> 보이게 해 준다.

as though(= as if)는 '마치 ~인 것처럼, 마치 ~인 듯이'라는 뜻이에요. 접속사이기 때문에 뒤에는 '주어 + 동사'가 따라와요. 또, 동사의 시제에 따라 의미가 달라요.

ex. He talks <u>as though</u> he knows everything. 그는 <u>마치</u> 모든 것을 알고 있는 <u>것처럼</u> 말한다. (현재: 실제로 아는 것 같음)

He talks <u>as though</u> he knew everything. 그는 <u>마치</u> 모든 것을 알고 있던 <u>것처럼</u> 말한다. (가정법 과거: 현재 사실과 반대. 실제로 모름)

Comprehension Quiz

A 빈칸에 알맞은 말을 골라 넣어 문장을 완성하세요.

blocks	tubes	types	sails

❶ There are three main _____________ of paint.

❷ Oil paints are stored in _____________ .

❸ Canvas is used for _____________ and tents.

❹ A watercolor tin contains _____________ of color.

B 밑줄 친 부분에 들어갈 알맞은 말에 동그라미 하세요.

❶ (Botanical / Abstract) artist Martin J. Allen paints highly detailed paintings of plants.

❷ Artists who paint (still life / abstract) art claim that they get their ideas as they go along.

❸ The artist chooses the (medium / mural) depending on how the finished piece will look, or what message will be given.

❹ Many artists choose to paint on a flat (tube / surface), which can later be hung on a wall for viewing.

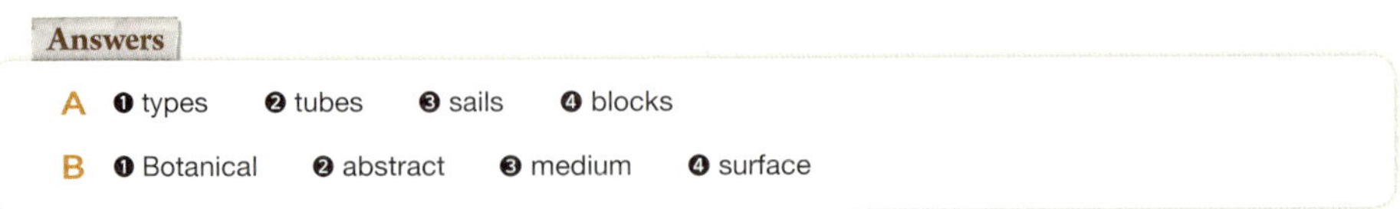

 다음 질문에 알맞은 답을 고르세요.

❶ What inspired the "black" paintings of Odilon Redon?

a) his illness

b) his blindness

c) his friendships

d) his dreams and nightmares

❷ Which of these is NOT a type of paint?

a) oil

b) canvas

c) watercolor

d) acrylic

D 다음 내용이 옳으면 T, 틀리면 F에 표시하세요.

❶ Acrylic paints were invented in the 19th century.　　T　F

❷ Acrylic paints are kept in tubes.　　T　F

❸ Acrylic paints can be used on very few surfaces.　　T　F

❹ Acrylic paints can be used for creating a picture with a rough texture.　　T　F

Answers

C　❶ d　　❷ b

D　❶ F　　❷ T　　❸ F　　❹ T

Painting a Picture

그림 그리기

Once the artist has decided what to paint, and which media will be used, it's time to decide *where* to work on the painting. An artist who wishes to paint a landscape may choose to go outside. He or she may sit or stand in front of the view they want to paint. If it is a scene that is unlikely to change over a period of days, and if the weather remains suitable, an artist may complete the whole picture outside.

- **scene** 장면, 현장
- **be unlikely to + 동사원형** ~할 것 같지 않다
- **period** 기간, 시기
- **remain** 여전히 ~이다, 남다, (해야 할 일 등이) 남아 있다
- **suitable** 적합한, 알맞은

More often, he or she makes a pencil sketch first, and may add bits of paint which have been mixed to the exact shade required. The artist may take photographs and add written notes to the sketch in order to remember exactly how the scene looked. Then, the artist goes back indoors to produce the actual painting.

Sometimes, an artist works entirely from a photograph. This has several advantages, such as the fact that the subject will remain completely the same. If an artist is painting a person or an animal, it can be easier to copy a photograph. The subject is not moving, complaining, or changing the way they look from one day to the next! However, some artists prefer to work from the original subject — the actual person or animal. They want their painting to capture the character as well as the way the subject looks.

- **more often (than not)** 자주, 대개
- **bits of** 약간의, 하찮은, 조그마한
- **exact** 정확한, 정밀한(*cf.* exactly 정확히)
- **note** (기억을 돕기 위한) 메모, 쪽지, 주석, 필기
- **in order to + 동사원형** ~하기 위하여
- **actual** 실제의, 사실상의
- **entirely** 전적으로, 완전히

- **advantage** 유리한 점, 장점
- **complain** 불평하다, 항의하다
- **from one day to the next** 하루하루(상황이 불확실하고 변화가 심한 경우를 나타냄)
- **prefer** ~을 더 좋아하다, 선호하다
- **character** 특징, 성격, (책·영화의) 등장인물, 글자

Many artists choose to paint indoors. Some artists use ordinary rooms in their homes. This requires careful thought because not just any room will do.  If an artist is going to paint a large painting, it may be set up on an easel, which takes up a lot of space. There may be a big mess to clean up, and sketches or photographs may be pinned up around the room. The artist needs a place where these things can be left out, rather than having to tidy them away each day.

- **ordinary** 보통의, 일상적인, 평범한
- **do** 적절하다, 충분하다, 하다
- **set up** ~을 세우다, ~을 설치하다(set-set-set)
- **easel** 이젤(작업하거나 전시하기 위해서 캔버스를 올려놓는 삼각대)
- **take up** (시간·공간을) 차지하다, 쓰다
- **space** (비어 있는·이용할 수 있는) 공간, 우주
- **pin up** ~을 핀으로 고정하다
- **rather than** ~보다는, ~ 대신에
- **have to + 동사원형** ~해야 한다
- **tidy away** (방 안이 깔끔해지도록) 치우다, 정리하다 (cf. tidy 정돈하다; 잘 정돈된)

Aha! English

This requires careful thought because not just any room will do. 이것은 세심한 생각을 요구하는데, 그냥 아무 방이나 되는 것이 아니기 때문이다.

'~ will do'는 뭔가가 특정한 목적을 충족시키거나 그 목적에 적합할 때 사용하는 표현으로, '~이면 충분하다[됐다]' 정도의 뜻이에요.

ex. I don't need any more pizza. One piece will do. 난 피자는 이제 됐다. 한 조각이면 충분하다.

The room needs plenty of natural light, so large windows are helpful. But light changes throughout the day. A room which receives a lot of warm sunlight in the morning may be darker and dimmer during the afternoon. Changes in light cause changes in the color of the subject and may also cast shadows. For this reason, some artists in the northern hemisphere choose a room that faces north. It receives less sunlight, but the light stays almost the same throughout the day.

- **light** 빛; (빛을) 비추다(light-lit-lit)
- **throughout** ~ 동안 죽, ~ 내내, 곳곳에
- **dim** 어둑한, 흐릿한, 침침한(*cf*. dimly 흐릿하게)
- **cause** 일으키다, 초래하다
- **cast a shadow** 그림자를 드리우다(cast-cast-cast)
- **for this reason** 이런 이유로
- **northern** 북쪽에 위치한, 북부의
- **hemisphere** (지구의) 반구, 반구체

▲ Joos van Craesbeeck(주 반 크레스벡)의 *The Painter's Studio*(화가의 작업실)

Some artists are lucky enough to have a room that is set aside just for their art, called a studio. They can go into their studio and escape from all the distractions of life to focus on their painting. So what should an artist's studio look like? Leonardo da Vinci said that the studio should be small, to help the artist to concentrate. Not everyone agrees. Pablo Picasso had a huge studio where many of his artworks were kept.  He also entertained models and visitors.

Aha! Culture

Montmartre & Picasso 몽마르트르와 피카소

몽마르트르는 프랑스 파리 북부에 있는 지역의 이름으로, 파리에서 가장 높은 언덕이에요. 이곳은 파리 중심부보다 집값이 싸서 20세기 초반 가난한 예술가들이 모여들어 살기 시작했어요. 피카소는 생전에 부와 명예를 얻은 예술가여서 원하는 대로 큰 작업실을 쓸 수 있었지만, 그런 그도 20대 초반 처음 파리에서 예술 활동을 시작했을 땐 몽마르트르 언덕의 가난한 예술가였답니다.

Some artists need a big studio because their paintings are big. Jackson Pollock, a U.S. artist who died in 1956, created huge paintings by laying his canvases on the floor and dripping or splashing paint all over them.

▲ Jackson Pollock(잭슨 폴록)의 작업실 바닥

A studio may not just be for painting. If an artist is going to spend hours working on something, there is often a small kitchen, a sofa or even a bed. Some artists can only work if their studio is tidy. But others are so busy creating that they don't notice the big mess around them.

POP QUIZ

Who created paintings by dripping paint onto canvases on the floor?

ⓐ Pablo Picasso
ⓑ Jackson Pollock

정답 ⓑ

- **set aside** 따로 떼어두다, (다시 필요할 때까지) ~을 한쪽으로 치워놓다, 챙겨두다
- **studio** (예술가들의) 작업실, (영화 촬영·방송국의) 스튜디오, 원룸 (아파트)
- **escape** 달아나다, 피하다, 탈출하다
- **distraction** (주의력) 집중을 방해하는 것, 오락
- **focus on** ~에 초점을 맞추다, 주력하다
- **concentrate** 집중하다, 집중시키다
- **entertain** (특히 집에서 손님을) 접대하다, 즐겁게 해 주다
- **lay** 놓다, 깔다, 설치하다(lay-laid-laid)
- **drip** 방울방울 떨어뜨리다, 방울방울 떨어지다
- **splash** (물·흙탕물 등을) 끼얹다, 튀기다, 후두두 떨어지다
- **notice** 알아차리다, 주목하다

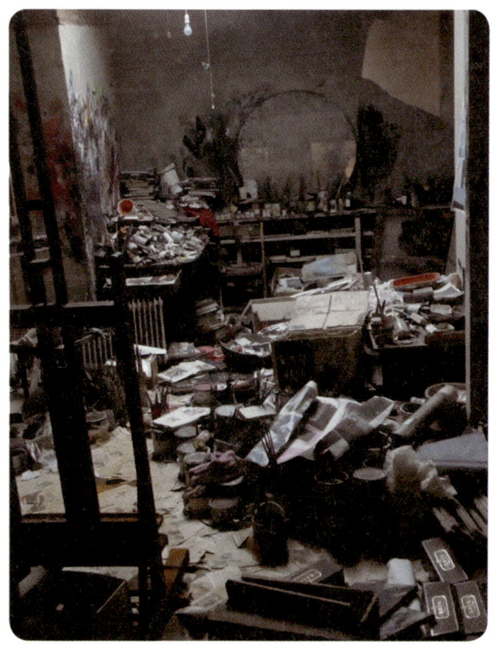

▲ 재현된 Francis Bacon(프랜시스 베이컨)의 작업실

Tourists in Dublin, Ireland, can go and visit a replica of the studio belonging to Irish-born painter Francis Bacon, who died in 1992. The floor is covered with tins of paint, photographs, articles cut from newspapers, and all kinds of objects.

Francis Bacon once said that he could not work in places that were too tidy.

He found it much easier to paint in a studio that was messy.

- **replica** 복제, 모형, 모조품, 복원물
- **Irish** 아일랜드의, 아일랜드인의; 아일랜드어, 아일랜드 사람
- **article** (신문·잡지·책의) 기사, 물품
- **be ready to + 동사원형** ~할 준비가 되어 있다, ~하기를 마다하지 않다
- **professional** 전문적인, 전문가의
- **ultramarine** 울트라마린, 군청색(의)
- **cobalt blue** 코발트 블루, 암청색
- **Prussian blue** 프러시안 블루, 감청색
- **pale** 연한, 엷은, 창백한
- **amount** 양, 액수, 총액
- **primary color** 원색
- **combination** 조합, 결합
- **purple** 자주색(의)
- **aim to + 동사원형** ~하는 것을 목표로 하다
- **intense** 강렬한, 격렬한, 짙은

▲ 여러 가지 푸른 색의 이름

Once the artist is ready to begin, he or she must choose which colors to use. Paint colors, whether they are oils, watercolors or acrylics, come in many different shades with interesting names. A professional artist's collection of paints will not simply contain "blue." It might include such exciting names as "ultramarine," "cobalt blue" and "Prussian blue." Of course, an artist may create whatever shades of color he or she wants by mixing paints together. Adding white will make a color paler. Adding tiny amounts of black will make it darker. Mixing the primary colors of red, blue, and yellow together in different combinations will produce shades of purple, orange, and green. Some painters of modern art focus only on one color. They aim to produce a new shade of that color which is particularly beautiful or intense.

The process of painting is different for each artist. Some spend hours getting a very small part of the painting perfect. Others create a general idea of the overall picture and then change parts of it. They add or change colors, and correct mistakes. Some people think that once the painting is done, it cannot be altered, but this is not true. Art historians use the term "pentimento" for paintings which suggest that the artist changed his or her mind about the painting while it was being painted. Sometimes this can be seen by experts, who notice that there are traces of paint which do not seem to match the finished picture. Often, these traces of the original picture are invisible until X-ray or infra-red technology is used to study the painting.

- **process** 과정, 절차, 공정
- **general** 대강의, 일반적인, 보통의
- **overall** 전반적인, 전체의
- **correct** 바로잡다, 정정하다; 맞는, 정확한
- **alter** 바꾸다, 고치다, 변하다
- **historian** 사학자, 역사가
- **term** 용어, 학기, 기간
- **pentimento** 펜티멘토(제작 도중에 변경하여 뭉개버린 형상이나 마무리 손질이 어렴풋이 남아 있는 자취, 또는 아련히 나타나는 원래의 형태)

- **suggest** 암시하다, 시사하다, 제안하다
- **expert** 전문가, 달인
- **trace** 흔적, 미량; 추적하다
- **seem** ~인 것처럼 보이다, ~인 것 같다
- **match** (색깔·무늬 등이) 어울리다, 일치하다, 맞먹다
- **invisible** 보이지 않는, 볼 수 없는(↔ visible)
- **infra-red** 적외선의
- **study** 조사하다, 검토하다, 공부하다

▲ Rembrandt(렘브란트)의 *The Syndics of the Amsterdam Drapers*(포목상 조합 이사들)

▲ 화가가 그린 초기의 인물 구도를 보여주는 위 그림의 엑스레이 영상

▲ Jan van Eyck(얀 반 에이크)의
The Arnolfini Portrait(아르놀피니 부부의 초상)

A good example of this is *The Arnolfini Portrait.* It was painted by Jan van Eyck in 1434. Scientific examination of the portrait has revealed the changes that Jan van Eyck made. The eyes, hands, and feet were originally in different positions. Most of these changes were made when the painting was just an "underdrawing." This means they were made before the paint was added. But some were made during the painting process itself.

Some changes are easier to make than others. When using acrylic paints, an artist can remove as much of the original as possible. Then the area may be painted with titanium white paint. This gives a white base on which to add the new color. With oil

paints, it is not so easy. Adding extra layers of paint may simply draw more attention to a mistake. But oil paint which is not yet dry may be removed using a soft cloth. A little linseed oil may be added to remove the final traces. Watercolor paints are soluble in water, so they can be re-wetted by adding more water. Then, they may be lifted off with an absorbent kitchen paper towel. Once the painting surface is dry again, the artist may continue painting with fresh paint.

POP QUIZ

How can we change an oil painting?
ⓐ use a soft cloth when it is not yet dry
ⓑ add more water

ⓔ 답정

- **underdrawing** (물감을 칠하기 전의) 밑그림, 소묘
- **titanium white** 티탄백(백색 안료, 그림물감)
- **base** 바탕, (사물의) 맨 아랫부분, 기초, 기반
- **layer** 층, 겹, 막
- **draw attention to** ~에 관심을 끌다
- **linseed oil** 아마인유(아마인 씨로 만든 오일)
- **soluble** (액체에) 녹는, 해결할 수 있는
- **lift** 제거하다, 들어 올리다, 들리다, 올라가다
- **absorbent** (특히 액체를) 잘 빨아들이는, 흡수력 있는

Chapter Three

Comprehension Quiz

A 빈칸에 알맞은 전치사를 골라 넣어 문장을 완성하세요.

around on in from

❶ Some artists are so busy creating that they don't notice the mess ______________ them.

❷ The floor is covered with articles cut ______________ newspapers.

❸ Francis Bacon said that he could not work ______________ places that were too tidy.

❹ An artist may spend hours working ______________ something.

B 밑줄 친 부분에 들어갈 알맞은 말에 동그라미 하세요.

❶ Oil paint which is not yet dry may be (painted / completed / removed) using a soft cloth.

❷ Watercolor paints are (soluble / solid / invisible) in water, so they can be re-wetted by adding more water.

❸ Watercolor paints may be lifted off with absorbent kitchen (paper towel / tools / brushes).

❹ Once the painting surface is dry again, the artist may (stop / cease / continue) painting with fresh paint.

Answers

A ❶ around ❷ from ❸ in ❹ on

B ❶ removed ❷ soluble ❸ paper towel ❹ continue

❶ Why is it an advantage to paint from a photograph instead of a real, living subject?

a) The artist can see more detail.

b) The painting is more realistic.

c) The subject is not moving.

d) The colors can be matched more accurately.

❷ As well as painting, what did Pablo Picasso do in his studio?

a) He framed pictures for other people.

b) He laid out all his canvases on the floor.

c) He entertained models and visitors.

d) He sold tickets for the public to come and view it.

D 관련 있는 것끼리 연결하여 문장을 완성하세요.

❶ An artist may create •

❷ Some painters of modern art •

❸ Some artists spend hours getting •

• a) focus only on one color.

• b) whatever shades of color he or she wants.

• c) a very small part of the painting perfect.

Answers

C ❶ c   ❷ c

D ❶ b   ❷ a   ❸ c

The Finished Painting

완성된 그림

At last, the painting is complete! Now, many more people with different jobs are needed to take the painting further on its journey.

The next stage is usually framing. This may be done by the artist if she or he knows how, but is often done by a picture framer. There are two main reasons for framing a finished painting. The first is to make it look attractive. The second is to protect it from damage.

Most paintings are displayed within a frame, but some modern canvases are displayed without a frame. This means that the sides of the painting are visible. Paintings done on paper or board are framed for support. Many paintings on canvas are framed, too. A canvas must first be stretched over wooden bars called stretcher bars, and the painting is fastened to the sides of the bars. Paper is much more fragile than canvas. It is usually mounted on some kind of board before framing, to prevent tearing or other damage.

▲ 틀에 고정된 캔버스

Name the bars used in preparing a canvas for framing.
ⓐ gallery bars
ⓑ stretcher bars

ⓑ 답정

- **further** (거리상) 더 멀리에(far의 비교급)
- **stage** 단계, 무대
- **frame** 틀에 넣다, 테를 두르다; 틀, 액자, 뼈대 (cf. framer 액자공, 액자 작업자)
- **attractive** 매력적인, 멋진
- **damage** 손상, 피해; 피해를 주다, 훼손하다
- **board** 판자, 널, 판지(= cardboard)
- **support** 버팀대, 지탱, 도움; 지지하다, 떠받치다

- **stretch** 늘이다, 펴다, (어떤 지역에 걸쳐) 뻗어 있다
- **stretcher** (미술용품) 캔버스 틀(캔버스 천을 당겨서 고정하는 틀)
- **fasten** (두 부분을 연결하여) 매다, 고정하다, 묶다, 채워지다
- **fragile** 부서지기 쉬운, 취약한, 허약한
- **mount** 부착하다(= attach), 탑재하다, 증가하다
- **prevent** 막다, 예방하다

Often, a painting is framed behind glass, especially if it is painted on paper. Glass keeps the painting in good condition by protecting it from dust or chemicals in the air. It prevents people from touching the painting. It also reduces the amount of light — especially ultraviolet light — that reaches the painting.  Although light is needed to view the painting and to appreciate its colors, too much light can damage the painting. This is why many art galleries are dimly lit.

POP QUIZ

What kind of light damages paintings most?

ⓐ ultraviolet light
ⓑ blue light

ⓔ 답정

- **dust** 먼지, 티끌, 가루
- **chemical** 화학 물질; 화학의, 화학적인
- **reduce** 줄이다, (가격 등을) 낮추다
- **ultraviolet light** 자외선
- **reach** ~에 이르다, 도달하다, (어떤 사람의 관심권 안에) 들어가다
- **appreciate** 감상하다, 진가를 알아보다, 고마워하다
- **instead** 대신에, 그보다는 오히려
- **varnish** 니스, 광택제, 유약; 니스를 칠하다, 광택을 내다
- **patient** 참을성 있는, 끈기 있는; 환자
- **crack** 균열, 깨진 틈, 딱 하는 소리
- **worthless** 가치 없는, 쓸모없는
- **occasionally** 가끔, 이따금
- **give protection to** ~을 보호하다
- **valuable** 소중한, 귀중한

Aha! Science

ultraviolet light & glass 자외선과 유리

자외선이란 무엇일까요? 태양은 다양한 파장을 가진 광선을 뿜어내요. 햇빛을 프리즘에 투과시키면

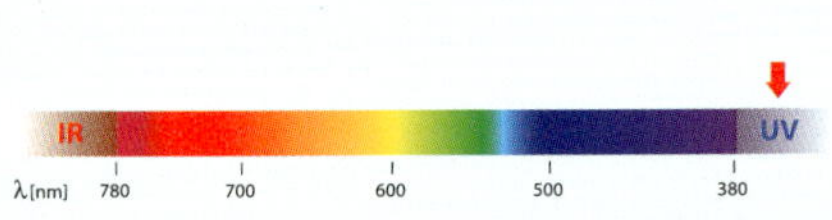

빨주노초파남보의 색을 띠는데, 이렇게 각기 다른 색으로 우리 눈에 보이는 선을 가시광선이라고 하죠. 자외선은 '보라색 밖에 있는' 광선이라는 뜻으로, 파장이 짧아 우리 눈에는 보이지 않아요. 자외선은 색을 변색 및 탈색시키기 때문에 미술 작품에는 치명적이지만 유리를 잘 투과하지 못하기 때문에 유리 액자 속 미술 작품을 보호할 수 있어요.

Oil paintings do not need glass to protect them. Instead, a layer of transparent varnish is added on top of the painting. This is where an artist needs to be very patient. An oil painting must only be varnished six months after it has been completed! This is to make sure that the paint is completely dry.  If the paint is very thick, the artist must wait even longer. If the varnish is added too soon, the varnish will dry before the paint does. After a while, cracks will appear on the surface. The painting will be worthless and the artist will find it difficult to make any money from it. Occasionally, oil paintings are framed under glass, particularly in museums and art galleries. This is usually to give protection to very valuable paintings that may be damaged by members of the public.

▲ 유화 표면의 균열

This is to make sure that the paint is completely dry. 이것은 물감이 <u>반드시</u> 완전히 마르도록 하기 위해서이다.

make sure는 '반드시[꼭] ~하다' 또는 '~을 확실히 하다'의 뜻이에요.

ex. <u>Make sure</u> that you turn the computer off. 꼭 컴퓨터를 꺼라.

The next decision is what kind of frame to use. Some frames are very thin and plain. Others are extremely elaborate, and are carved or molded into fancy shapes. Frames are traditionally made of wood, but in modern times they may also be made of metal or certain plastics. Some frames are "gilded." This means that they are made to look as though they are made of gold. This can be done by painting them with gold paint or by adding gold leaf. Gold leaf is an extremely thin layer of real gold, added little by little with a fine brush.

▲ 액자 제작에 사용되는 금박

▲ 액자에 금박을 입히는 모습

- **plain** 소박한, 분명한, 있는 그대로의
- **extremely** 극도로, 극히, 매우
- **elaborate** 정교한, 공을 들인
- **carve (into)** (~으로) 조각하다, (~에) 새기다
- **mold** 틀에 넣어 만들다, 본뜨다
- **fancy** 복잡한, 장식이 많은, 색깔이 화려한, 값비싼

- **traditionally** 전통적으로, 예전부터
- **metal** 금속; 금속의
- **certain** 특정한, 어떤, 확실한
- **gild** 금(박)을 입히다, 도금하다
- **gold leaf** (장식용) 금박
- **fine** 고운, 촘촘한, 질 높은, 좋은

When the framing is complete, the painting is ready to be displayed and put up for sale. At this point, the artist may need the help of several people. They can help to sell his or her paintings and to reach the

widest audience. Of course, artists can sell their own work. But it takes a lot of time and effort that could be used for painting more pictures. For this reason, many artists choose to use the services of an agent.

An art agent is someone who works on behalf of artists to get their work displayed in the right places and sold to the right people. The agent is usually someone who has many years of experience in the art world. The agent has a lot of connections with buyers, galleries and auction houses (which we will talk about in the next chapter).

POP QUIZ

What is correct about an art agent?

ⓐ An art agent sells his or her own paintings.
ⓑ An art agent has many years of experience in the art world.

정답 ⓑ

- **put up for sale** 팔려고 내놓다, 경매에 부치다
- **audience** 관람객, 청중, 시청자, 독자, 팬들
- **agent** 중개상, 대리인
- **on behalf of** ~을 대신하여, ~을 위하여
- **connection** 연줄이 닿는 사람[기관], 관련성, 연결
- **auction house** 경매 전문 회사

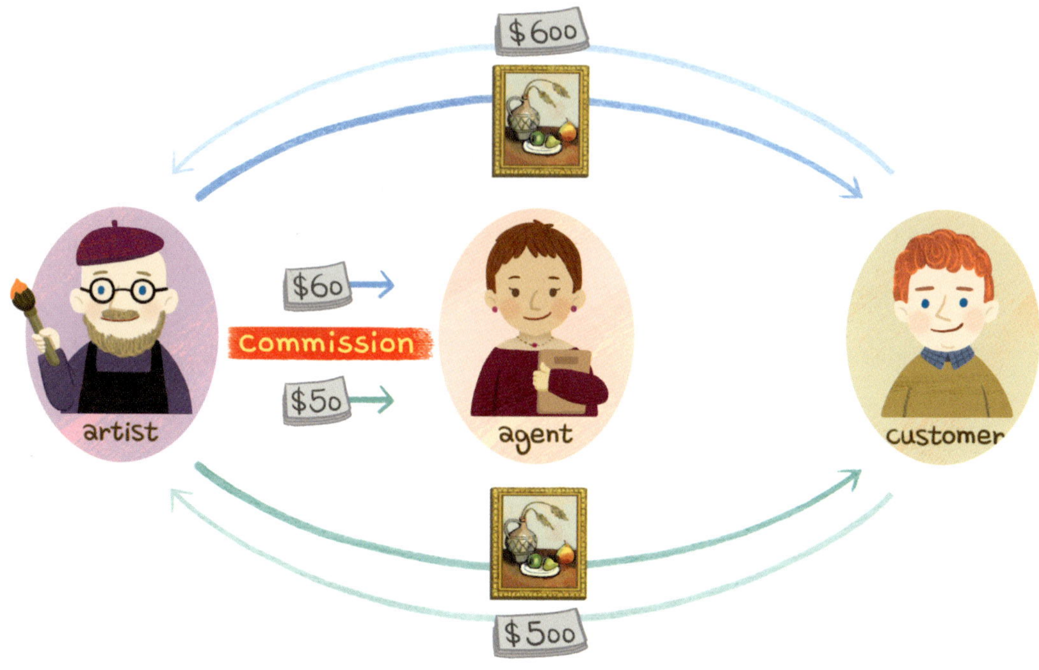

The agent makes his or her money by taking a percentage
of the money that the artist earns. This is called working for
"commission." It means that the more money the artist makes,
the more money the agent makes! Some agents, instead of
working on behalf of the artist, work on behalf of a gallery. They
look around for suitable artworks to display and sell. They may
contact artists to ask if they have any work currently ready
to display. Many agents who work this way are experts in a
particular style of art. They often travel all over the world to find
new and exciting artists.

Artists who are already quite well-known and successful may use the services of an art manager. Many musicians such as pop stars use managers to arrange everything in their careers. The art manager does a similar thing for the artist. The manager takes care of all the artist's business. Money management, marketing, and publicity events are some of the things a manager may take care of.

Of course, an artist who is just beginning a career in painting may not have an agent, and certainly will not have a manager. The artist needs to get his or her paintings in front of people who may enjoy looking at them and may even want to buy them. The best way to do this is to hold an exhibition in an art gallery.

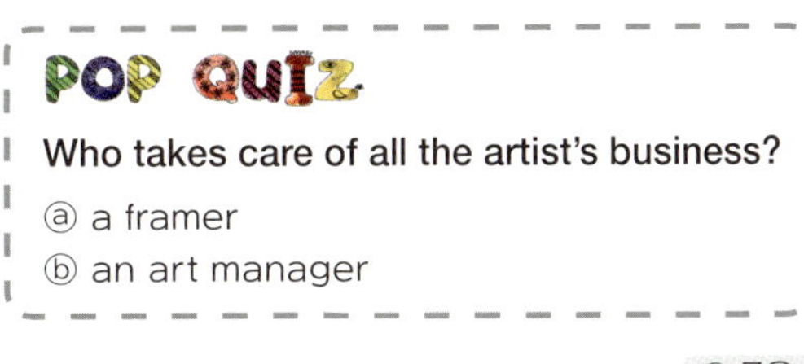

- **earn** (돈을) 벌다, (이자·수익 등을) 얻다
- **commission** (위탁 판매 ·은행 서비스 등의 대가로 받는) 수수료, 위원회
- **contact** 접촉하다, 연락하다
- **currently** 현재, 지금
- **career** 직업, 경력, 직장 생활
- **similar** 비슷한, 닮은

- **management** 관리, 운영, 경영
- **marketing** 마케팅(홍보·운송·보관·판매 등의 상품 유통에 관계되는 활동 전반)
- **publicity** 홍보, 광고, 널리 알림
- **event** 행사, (특히 중요한) 사건, (스포츠 대회 중에 진행되는 하나의) 경기
- **hold an exhibition** 전시회를 개최하다

Chapter Four

Comprehension Quiz

A 알맞은 것끼리 연결하여 문장을 완성하세요.

❶ An artist　　　　　　　　a) displays the picture to the public.

❷ An agent　　　　　　　　b) manages the artist's business.

❸ An art manager　　　　　c) paints the picture.

❹ A gallery　　　　　　　　d) tries to sell work for a commission.

B 빈칸에 알맞은 말을 골라 넣어 문장을 완성하세요.

worthless	suitable	visible	transparent

❶ When canvases are displayed without a frame, the sides are ____________.

❷ A layer of ____________ varnish is added on top of oil paintings.

❸ A painting with cracks on the surface will be ____________.

❹ Art agents look around for ____________ artworks to display and sell.

Answers

A ❶ c　❷ d　❸ b　❹ a

B ❶ visible　❷ transparent　❸ worthless　❹ suitable

C 다음 질문에 알맞은 답을 고르세요.

❶ What is a "gilded" frame?

a) a frame that is thin and plain

b) a frame that is carved from one piece of wood

c) a frame that is made of pure gold

d) a frame that is made to look as though it is made of gold

❷ Why do many artists choose NOT to sell their own work by themselves?

a) They would rather spend their time painting.

b) They do not think it is good enough to sell.

c) They are not interested in making money.

d) They do not know anyone to sell it to.

D 다음 내용이 옳으면 T, 틀리면 F에 표시하세요.

❶ All agents work on behalf of an artist. T F

❷ An agent usually has a lot of experience in the art world. T F

❸ Many agents travel all over the world. T F

❹ The less money an artist makes, the more money an agent makes. T F

Answers

C ❶ d   ❷ a

D ❶ F   ❷ T   ❸ T   ❹ F

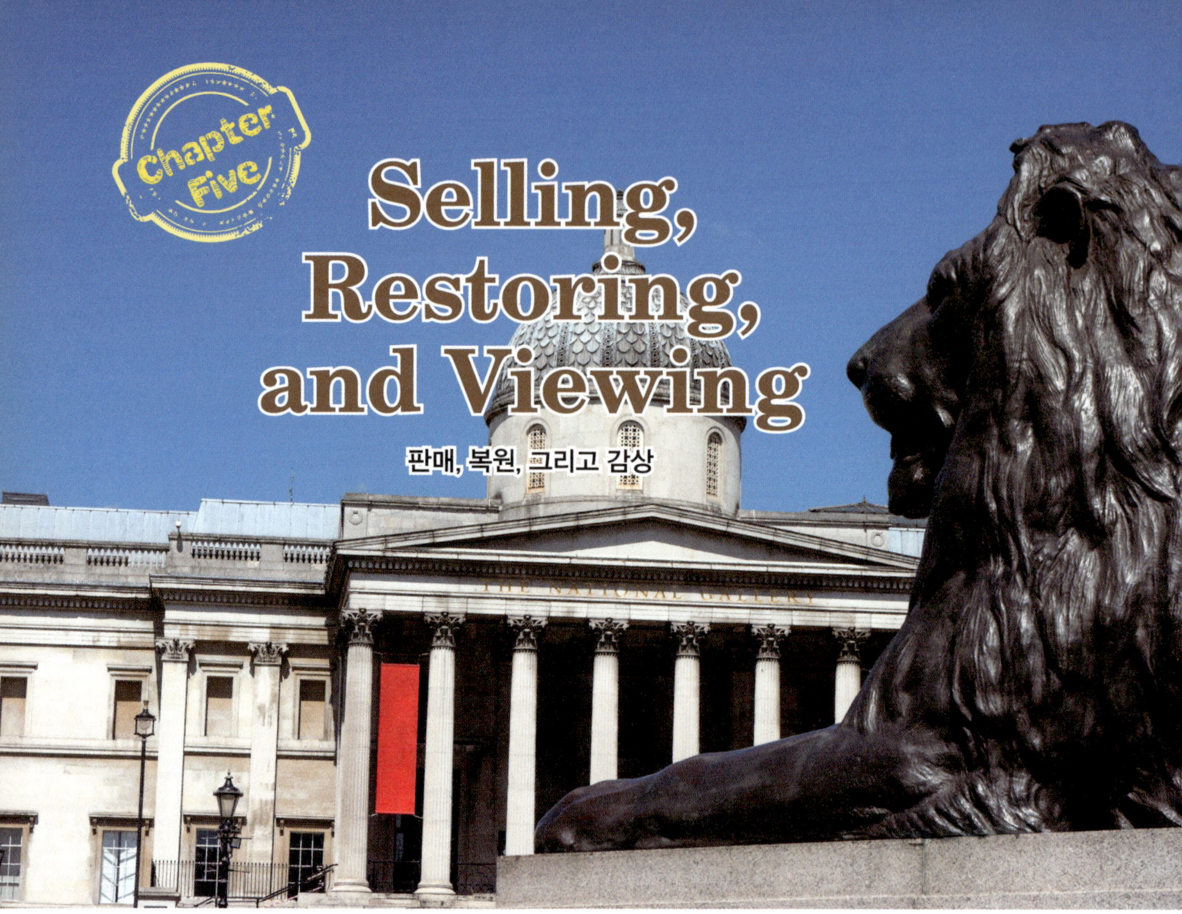

Selling, Restoring, and Viewing

판매, 복원, 그리고 감상

Galleries are rooms or buildings with plenty of space for displaying artworks such as paintings. They are open to allow viewers to come and look at the paintings. Even the fictional spy James Bond visits art galleries! In the 2012 movie, *Skyfall*, James Bond meets his boss, Q, in the National Gallery, London.

- **fictional** 허구적인, 소설의
- **boss** (직장의) 상관, 상사, 사장
- **national** 국립의, 국가 소유의, 국가의
- **feature** 출연하다; 특색, 특성
- **naughty** 버릇없는, 말을 안 듣는

- **pearl earring** 진주 귀고리
- **offer for sale** 팔려고 내놓다
- **attend** 참석하다, 다니다
- **along with** ~와 함께, 더불어
- **occasion** 특별한 행사, (어떤 일이 일어나는 특정한) 때, 기회

The same gallery features in the 2007 movie, *St. Trinian's*, about a group of very naughty schoolgirls who steal a famous painting called *Girl with a Pearl Earring*. This is a public gallery, where the work is not for sale. Smaller galleries hold special events or exhibitions, where the work of a particular artist may be displayed and offered for sale.

▲ Johannes Vermeer(요하네스 페르메이르)의 *Girl with a Pearl Earring*(진주 귀고리를 한 소녀)

Usually, there is a special event on the first night of the exhibition. The artist attends, along with invited guests who may buy the paintings. Food and drink are usually served, and it is an exciting social occasion.

Girl with a Pearl Earring 진주 귀고리를 한 소녀

네덜란드의 화가 요하네스 페르메이르가 1665년경에 그린 작품이에요. 그는 푸른색과 노란색을 쓰기를 좋아했는데, 그 특성이 이 작품에도 잘 나타나고 있죠. 어두운 배경 앞에서 관람객 쪽을 돌아보고 있는 소녀의 얼굴은 많은 이야기를 담고 있는 듯한 묘한 표정을 띠고 있어서 어떤 사람들은 이 소녀를 '네덜란드의 모나리자'라고 부르기도 해요. 이국적인 터번을 두르고 진주 귀고리를 한 이 소녀의 모델이 누구인지는 알려지지 않았어요.

If an artist exhibits his or her work in a gallery, hopefully people will come and buy the work. Sometimes, they do not buy the work immediately, especially if the price is high. The artist needs a catalog. This is a glossy magazine-style book with images of the paintings in it, and details of prices. Customers may take these catalogs away and take time to make their decision.

Some customers may want to buy a painting simply because they like looking at it, and would love to see it hanging in their home. Other customers buy a painting because they collect art and they see it as an investment. This means that they will only buy a painting that they think will be worth even more money in the future. Such customers will be especially interested in finding out more about the artist. They have to decide whether to invest in both the artist and the work. For this reason, artists who are serious about making a living from their painting need to have a website. Here, they can give information about themselves and their work.

There is another important job in the art world, which helps customers to decide whether to buy a painting or not. This is the job of the art critic.  An art critic is someone who looks at art and thinks about how well it has been painted. Critics give their opinions about all kinds of artworks. They write about art in magazines, newspapers, exhibition catalogs, and websites. Customers read the comments written by critics. They use the comments to help with the decision about what to buy.

POP QUIZ

What is a critic's job?
ⓐ read comments and buy paintings
ⓑ give opinions about artworks

ⓑ 답정

- **immediately** 즉시, 즉각
- **glossy** 화려한, 광이 나는; 고급 잡지
- **make one's decision** 결정하다
- **investment** 투자, 투자금
- **worth** 가치가 있는
- **find out** 알아내다, 알게 되다

- **invest in** ~에 투자하다
- **serious** 진지한, 심각한
- **make a living** 생계를 유지하다, 살아가다
- **critic** 비평가, 평론가
- **opinion** 의견, 견해
- **comment** 논평, 언급, 비판; 논평하다, 견해를 밝히다

🌐 Aha! Culture

art critic 미술 비평가

미술 비평가는 미술 작품을 분석하고 해석하며 평가하는 일을 하는 사람이에요. 미술 비평을 하려면 예술에 대한 심미안은 물론 미술사 전반에 대한 해박한 지식이 필요하죠. 하지만 많은 예술가들은 시대의 유행을 앞서나간 탓에 당대의 비평가들에게 좋지 못한 평가를 받는 일도 많았어요. 어떤 비평가들은 특정 미술 운동을 적극적으로 소개하고 예술가들을 옹호하면서 특정 미술 양식이 널리 퍼지는 것을 돕기도 해요.

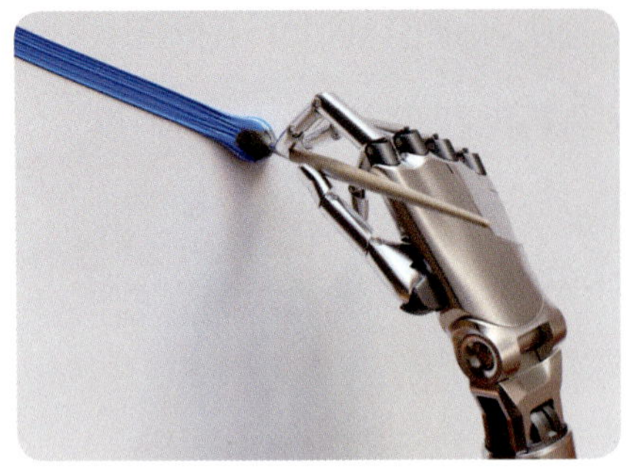

An unusual task for art critics took place in 2016 for the first time, when some critics judged the entries in the first annual robotic art competition. Open to teams from all over the world, this competition offers prizes worth $100,000 for artworks produced by robots! Robots can paint in two ways. Humans may operate a robotic arm using a remote control, or the robot may be controlled using computer software. One of the simplest techniques is for the robot to copy a photograph or painting. It paints one color at a time, so, for example, all the red parts of the picture may be painted first. Then, all the blue parts, the yellow parts, and so on. In this way, the picture is slowly built up.

- **take place** 개최되다, 일어나다
- **judge** 판단하다, 심사하다, 관결하다; 판사, 심판
- **entry** 출품작, 참가, 응모, 기재 사항
- **annual** 연간의, 매년의
- **competition** 대회, 시합, 경쟁
- **offer** 제공하다, 내놓다, 제안하다; 제안
- **operate** 작동하다, 가동되다, 영업하다
- **remote control** 원격 조종, 리모컨
- **and so on** 기타 등등(= and so forth)
- **build up** ~을 만들다, ~을 조성하다, ~을 증강하다

 **Aha! Culture**

The Robotic Art Competition 로봇 미술 경연대회

2016년에 제1회 로봇 미술 경연대회가 개최되었어요. 그림을 그리는 주체는 인공지능 로봇이되, 도구는 반드시 붓을 사용해야 한다는 규칙이었죠. 전 세계 총 15팀의 로봇 인공지능 연구팀이 모여들어 그림 실력을 겨루었는데, 우승을 한 팀은 다양한 색을 섞어 멋진 정물화를 그려낸 국립 타이완대학팀이었다고 합니다.

Another way of selling paintings is through art "auction houses."
Auction houses sell all kinds of items. In galleries, the price of
a painting is fixed. An auction is different. It is a special type
of sale where people decide what they would like to pay. An
expert seller called an "auctioneer" displays the painting to a

gathered crowd. The auctioneer
asks what people would like to
offer, or "bid." People who are
interested in buying the painting
raise their hand or nod their
head. This tells the auctioneer
that they want to compete with
the other buyers.

Who sells the paintings at an auction house?
ⓐ a bidder
ⓑ an auctioneer

ⓑ 답정

- **fixed** 고정된, 변치 않는
- **auctioneer** 경매사, 경매인
- **gather** 모이다, 모으다, 이해하다
- **crowd** (특정한) 집단, 군중, 일반 대중
- **bid** (특히 경매에서) 값을 부르다, 입찰에 응하다
  (bid-bid-bid); 호가(팔거나 사려는 물건의 값을 부름),
  가격 제시, 응찰, 노력

- **raise one's hand** 손을 들다
- **nod one's head** 고개를 끄덕이다
- **compete with** ~와 경쟁하다, (경기 등에서)
  ~와 겨루다, 참가하다

Each time, the bid increases and the price of the painting goes up. As the price gets higher, some bidders drop out of the competition. The auctioneer continues to ask for bids until only two or three bidders are left. Eventually, the painting is sold to the person who bids the highest price.

Two of the most famous art auction houses in the world are Christie's and Sotheby's.  They sell all kinds of art that you can imagine. Both of these auction houses operate all over the world, with famous salesrooms in London and New York.

In 2010, a painting by Pablo Picasso called *Nude, Green Leaves and Bust* was offered for sale by Christie's. It was sold in 8 minutes for the incredible sum of $106.5 million. Picasso painted this picture in a single day. That's a good rate of pay for one day's work! Picasso was wealthy when he died. But he'd still be amazed at that rate of pay.

Where was *Nude, Green Leaves and Bust* sold?
ⓐ Christie's
ⓑ Sotheby's

ⓔ 吕&

- **bidder** 가격 제시자, 응찰자
- **drop out of** ~에서 중도에 하차하다, 이탈하다
- **eventually** 결국, 마침내
- **salesroom** 경매장, 매장
- **bust** 상반신, 흉상

- **sum** 액수, 총계
- **in a single day** 단 하루에
- **rate of pay** 급료, 급여
- **be amazed at** ~에 깜짝 놀라다

▲ 런던의 소더비 경매장

▲ 소더비 경매 모습

Aha! Culture

Christie's & Sotheby's 크리스티 & 소더비

크리스티와 소더비는 모두 영국에서 시작된 세계 최고의 경매 회사예요. 크리스티는 미술품 판매, 소더비는 중고서적 판매에서 시작해서 명화, 조각, 보석, 와인 등 다양한 물건들을 파는 경매 회사가 되었죠. 이 두 회사는 모두 미술품을 감정하는 데 필요한 전문지식을 쌓기 위한 미술교육원을 운영하며 최고의 전문 경매사들을 배출하고 있어요. 최근 들어 소더비는 온라인을 통한 경매를 시작했어요. 그에 반해 크리스티는 여전히 전통적인 방식의 경매를 고수하고 있다고 해요.

An auction house, however, is not a place where new artists
generally sell their paintings. Many of the paintings sold
at auction houses are by well-known artists. Sometimes,
customers may build up a collection of paintings over many
years as an investment. Then, they may sell some or all of their
paintings at auction houses to make money. Two men called
Ezra and David Nahmad own the most valuable art collection
in the world. 🌐 It is valued at around $3 billion! Their collection
is stored in a warehouse near Geneva airport, in Switzerland.
This suggests that they do not buy the art because they love to
look at it. However, they make a lot of money from it and are the
most frequent sellers of art at Christie's in New York.

- **generally** 일반적으로, 대개
- **be valued at** ~의 가치로 평가되다
- **billion** 10억, 엄청난 양
- **warehouse** 창고, 도매점
- **frequent** 잦은, 빈번한

- **billionaire** 억만장자, 갑부
- **lend out** (돈을 받고) 빌려주다(lend-lent-lent)
- **hide away** (물건을) 숨기다, (몸을) 숨기다
- **bring out** 세상에 내놓다, 갖고 나가다

🌐 Aha! Culture

Ezra & David Nahmad 에스라 나마드 & 데이비드 나마드

이 둘은 형제로, 레바논 출신의 억만장자들이에요. 은행가였던 형제들의 아
버지는 안전을 위해 중동 지역을 떠나 이탈리아 밀라노로 가족들을 이주시켰
어요. 그때 나마드 형제들은 십대였는데, 이때부터 이미 학교를 빼먹고 미술
품을 보러 다니기 일쑤였다고 해요. 그들의 역사적인 미술품 컬렉션이 시작
된 것은 16세 때였어요. 어느 날 그들은 후안 그리스라는 화가의 전시회에 가
서 작품 두 점을 샀어요. 당시 후안 그리스의 작품은 아직 고가에 거래되지
않았었지만, 나중에 수십억대에 거래되는 작품으로 평가받게 되죠. 이렇게
투자할 가치가 있는 작품을 사들이기 시작한 두 형제는 전 세계적으로 유명
한 미술품 거래상이 되었답니다.

▲ Juan Gris(후안 그리스)의
정물화

Another great art collector is an American billionaire called Eli Broad, who owns 8,000 artworks. He wants these to be enjoyed by as many people as possible, so he lends out his paintings to galleries, museums, and universities.

▲ 브로드 미술관

So, in the same way that art is created for many different reasons, it is also bought for different reasons. How do artists feel when the painting that they have worked so hard on is hidden away and only brought out to make money? It is difficult to know, since many of the paintings which sell for the highest amounts are by artists who died many years ago. Fortunately, many of them are displayed for anyone to see in public art galleries.

Eli Broad 일라이 브로드

1933년 미국 뉴욕에서 태어난 일라이 브로드는 다수의 성공한 사업체를 보유한 사업가이자 미술 수집가예요. 그는 가난한 가정에서 태어났지만, 특유의 수완으로 막대한 재산을 가진 자산가가 되었죠. 2015년에 로스앤젤레스에서 개장한 브로드 미술관은 로스앤젤레스를 현대 미술의 본거지로 만들고 싶었던 일라이 브로드의 희망에서 시작되었어요. 사람들이 쉽게 찾아갈 수 있는 도심에 막대한 가치를 지닌 미술품들을 전시함으로써 자신이 가진 부를 사회에 환원하고자 했던 것이죠. 그는 많은 돈을 번 것으로도 유명하지만, 그만큼 많은 돈을 기부하는 것으로도 유명해요. 그는 자신의 남은 재산 중 75%를 앞으로 더 기부할 예정이라고 해요.

Some of the paintings displayed in public galleries are centuries old. They need the attention of some more important people in the art world. These people are curators and conservators. The art curator's job is to create and care for a collection of art for public display. The curator of a major public gallery decides which paintings to buy. He or she also decides which ones to hang on the walls, which to store carefully for a while, and which to lend to other galleries. The curator's job includes keeping careful records about the paintings. It also includes producing labels, written information, and catalog entries.

- **curator** 큐레이터(박물관·미술관 등의 전시 책임자)
- **conservator** (유적·예술품 등의) 문화재 보존가, 보존 처리 전문가, 후견인
- **care for** ~을 돌보다, ~을 아주 좋아하다
- **major** 주요한, 중대한
- **label** (종이 등에 물건에 대한 정보를 적어 붙여 놓은) 표, 상표
- **catalog entry** 카탈로그에 게재된 그림들의 소개 글

- **security guard** 경비원, 보안요원
- **get rid of** ~을 제거하다, 처리하다
- **accidentally** 우연히, 뜻하지 않게
- **ruin** 망치다, 폐허로 만들다
- **horrified** 겁에 질린, 공포감을 주는, 섬뜩한
- **lose** 잃어버리다, 패하다(lose-lost-lost)
- **be responsible for** ~에 책임이 있다

The 1997 comedy movie, *Bean*, features the curator of an art gallery in Los Angeles, whose name is David Langley. David believes Mr. Bean is a famous art critic sent by the National Gallery in London. So he invites him to stay at his house. But the National Gallery only sent Mr. Bean, a security guard, to get rid of him. When Mr. Bean accidentally ruins a famous and valuable painting called *Whistler's Mother,* David is horrified. He knows that he may lose his job, since he is responsible for taking care of the paintings. Being a curator is a very responsible job!

▲ James Whistler(제임스 휘슬러)의 *Whistler's Mother*(휘슬러의 어머니)

Whistler's Mother 휘슬러의 어머니

사실 이 그림의 진짜 이름은 〈휘슬러의 어머니〉가 아니라 *Arrangement in Grey and Black* 〈회색과 검은색의 구성〉이랍니다. 제목에서도 알 수 있듯이, 휘슬러가 이 그림에서 주인공으로 삼은 것은 벽과 기튼, 액자, 인물과 같은 구성물들과 그 색의 조화였지 '어머니'가 아니었어요. 하지만 이 작품이 미국에 알려졌을 때 미국인들은 검소하고 엄격한 자신들의 어머니를 떠올리며 감동했고, 그림 자체도 〈휘슬러의 어머니〉로 알려지게 되었어요.

The work of art conservators is more technical. Firstly, they conserve art. This means that they protect it against harm or damage. They try to keep it as close to its original condition as possible. They also repair artworks which have been damaged.

They are restored — brought back — to their original condition. The damage may have been done by age or by environmental issues such as water or light. Sometimes the restoration of a painting might actually cause more damage. Even if the restoration is carefully carried out, people might not like the result. 

Aha! English

Even if the restoration is carefully carried out, people might not like the result.
복원이 조심스럽게 행해지더라도, 사람들은 그 결과를 좋아하지 않을 수도 있다.

even if는 '(비록) ~한다고 해도'라는 뜻으로 어떤 상황을 가정하여 추측할 때 쓸 수 있어요. even if 문장 다음에는 추측의 문장이 이어진다는 것을 기억하세요.

ex. Even if you leave right now, you might not catch the train. 네가 지금 당장 떠난다고 해도, 그 기차를 타지 못할 수도 있다.

Art restoration should only be done by experts. In a small town in Spain called Zaragoza, there is a church with a fresco, which is a wall painting. The fresco is a painting of Jesus, and it is hundreds of years old. An eighty-year-old woman in the town noticed that white patches had developed on the face of Jesus, so she decided to fix it herself. She painted a new face of Jesus over the old one. Unfortunately, the new face looked completely different! But it is now a popular tourist attraction.

- **technical** 전문적인, 기술의
- **conserve** 보존하다, 보호하다, 아끼다
- **harm** 해, 피해, 손해; 해치다, 손상시키다
- **close** (시간적·공간적으로) 가까운, 친밀한
- **repair** 수선하다, 수리하다; 수리, 수선
- **restore** (이전의 상황·감정으로) 회복시키다, 복원하다
  (*cf.* restoration 복원, 복구)
- **bring back** ~을 회복시키다, ~을 상기시키다
- **environmental** 환경의, 환경과 관련된
- **issue** 문제, 쟁점
- **carry out** ~을 수행하다, 완수하다
- **fresco** 프레스코 벽화(덜 마른 회벽에 물에 갠 안료로 채색한 그림), 프레스코 화법
- **patch** 부분, 조각
- **tourist attraction** 관광 명소

When a painting is correctly restored, there is often a lot of science involved. Lasers can be used to remove dirt. They heat and expand the surface layer. This creates a wave of pressure which lifts dirt off the surface. The laser beam is only used for short amounts of time — often less than one second — but it is very powerful. Some art restorers use bacteria to clean

paintings. Certain bacteria produce chemicals called enzymes. The enzymes break down dirt and lift it off the surface of the painting without causing any damage.

- **dirt** 먼지, 때, 흙
- **expand** 팽창시키다, 팽창되다
- **pressure** 압력, 압박, 부담
- **enzyme** 효소
- **break down** ~을 분해하다, ~을 부수다, 고장 나다, 부서지다(break-broke-broken)

- **be at an end** 끝나다, (돈 등이) 떨어지다
- **most of all** 그중에서도, 무엇보다도
- **why not~?** (제안) ~하는 게 어떤가?
- **with enjoyment** 즐겁게, 즐기며
- **see if** ~인지 확인하다, ~일지 두고 보다
- **guess** (추측으로) 알아맞히다, 짐작하다

Aha! Science

enzymes 효소

효소란 생명 유지에 필요한 여러 화학 반응이 일어나게 해주는 촉매제예요. 모든 살아 있는 동물과 식물에 함유되어 있고, 그 종류가 천 가지가 넘는다고 하죠. 효소는 항균, 해독, 살균, 소화, 분해, 배출 등 우리 몸속에서 일어나는 여러 작용 전반에 걸쳐서 중요한 역할을 해요. 우리가 아주 잘 알고 있는 효소는 아밀레이스, 즉 침 속에 함유된 소화 효소예요. 음식물 속의 녹말을 분해해주는 역할을 하죠. 미술품 복원 전문가들도 그림의 표면이 약해 약품이나 물을 함부로 쓸 수 없을 때 바로 이 아밀레이스를 사용하기도 한답니다.

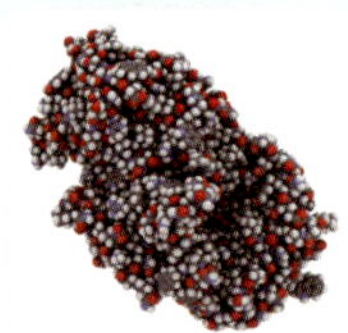

▲ 아밀레이스 원자

Now the journey of the painting is at an end. It has been painted, framed, sold, and displayed so that many people may enjoy looking at it. Why not take a trip to an art gallery to view some paintings? Or why not try painting a picture yourself and having it framed? Next time you look at a painting, think about all the people that have been involved in creating it. But most of all, look at it with enjoyment. See if you can guess the message that the artist wanted to give. That message has traveled a long way to reach you!

Comprehension Quiz

A 다음 문장이 어떤 장소에 대한 설명인지 골라 동그라미 하세요.

❶ The price of a painting is fixed.

GALLERY / AUCTION HOUSE

❷ People who want to buy a painting make a bid.

GALLERY / AUCTION HOUSE

❸ Customers must decide at once whether to buy a painting.

GALLERY / AUCTION HOUSE

❹ Customers may decide to buy a painting at a later date.

GALLERY / AUCTION HOUSE

B 다음 문장이 어떤 직업에 대한 설명인지 골라 동그라미 하세요.

❶ Produces labels and written information about paintings.

CURATOR / CONSERVATOR

❷ Repairs artworks that have been damaged.

CURATOR / CONSERVATOR

❸ Uses science to restore paintings to their original condition.

CURATOR / CONSERVATOR

❹ Decides which painting to hang on the walls.

CURATOR / CONSERVATOR

Answers

A	❶ GALLERY	❷ AUCTION HOUSE	❸ AUCTION HOUSE	❹ GALLERY
B	❶ CURATOR	❷ CONSERVATOR	❸ CONSERVATOR	❹ CURATOR

C 다음 질문에 알맞은 답을 고르세요.

❶ How do customers at an auction show that they want to make a bid?

a) They press buttons on a computer.

b) They raise their hands or nod their heads.

c) They call out the price they want to pay.

d) They stand up.

❷ Where do Ezra and David Nahmad store their art collection?

a) in a bank b) in a warehouse

c) in a gallery d) in a basement

D 빈칸에 알맞은 말을 골라 넣어 문장을 완성하세요.

invited	social	first	smaller

❶ _______________ galleries hold special events and exhibitions.

❷ Usually, there is a special event on the _______________ night of an exhibition.

❸ The artist attends, along with _______________ guests.

❹ This is an exciting _______________ occasion.

Answers

C ❶ b ❷ b

D ❶ Smaller ❷ first ❸ invited ❹ social

Let's Review the Story

빈칸을 채우며 이야기를 다시 정리해 보세요.

Title: ______________

Chapter 1

People create art for different reasons, e.g:
- to show which t __________ they belong to
- to make m __________
- to pass on a m __________

Chapter 2

Artists may use three different types of paint, which are:
- o __________
- w __________
- a __________

Chapter 3

Many artists work on their paintings in a s __________. This needs plenty of n __________ l __________. There may be a kitchen and a sofa or even a bed.

Chapter 4

Artists needs the help of other people:
- F __________ frame paintings to p __________ them and to make them look a __________.
- A __________ help artists to s __________ their artworks, and receive c __________ as payment.

Chapter 5

When paintings are sold, more people get involved:
- C __________ write about their o __________ of artworks.
- C __________ take care of art collections in public g __________.
- C __________ protect and r __________ paintings to their original condition.

아래의 물음에 대해 생각해 보고 자유롭게 답하세요.

❶ 여러분은 미술 작품을 감상하거나 직접 창작하는 것을 좋아하나요?
좋아한다면 왜 좋아하는지, 싫어한다면 왜 싫어하는지 이야기해 보세요.

❷ 본문에서는 미술 작품에 관련되는 다양한 사람들이 소개되었어요. 화가,
미술 중개인, 매니저, 미술 비평가, 경매사, 미술품 수집가, 큐레이터,
미술품 복원 전문가가 하는 일이 각각 어떻게 다른지 이야기해 보세요.

❸ 하나의 위대한 작품이 탄생하려면 화가 이외에 어떤 직업의 역할이 가장
중요할까요? 이유와 함께 이야기해 보세요.

❹ 본문에서 소개된 많은 화가의 작품 중에서, 가장 인상적인 것은 무엇인가
요? 왜 그렇게 생각하는지 이유와 함께 이야기해 보세요.

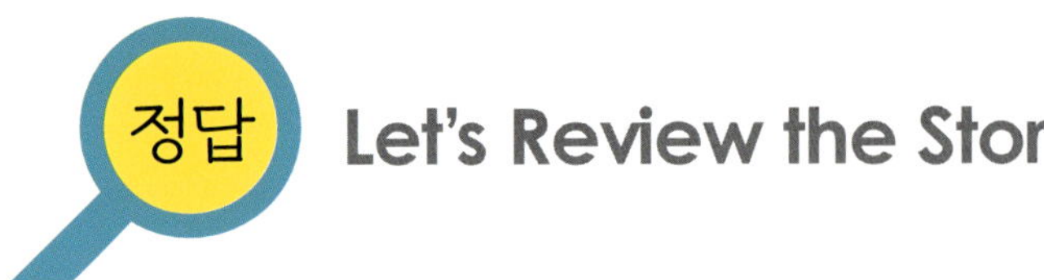

Let's Review the Story

Title: Things to Know about Paintings

Chapter 1
People create art for different reasons, e.g:
- to show which tribe they belong to
- to make money
- to pass on a message

Chapter 2
Artists may use three different types of paint, which are:
- oil
- watercolor
- acrylic

Chapter 3
Many artists work on their paintings in a studio . This needs plenty of natural light . There may be a kitchen and a sofa or even a bed.

Chapter 4
Artists needs the help of other people:
- Framers frame paintings to protect them and to make them look attractive .
- Agents help artists to sell their artworks, and receive commissions as payment.

Chapter 5
When paintings are sold, more people get involved:
- Critics write about their opinions of artworks.
- Curators take care of art collections in public galleries .
- Conservators protect and restore paintings to their original condition.

Things to Know about Paintings
전문 번역

그림에 관해 알아야 할 것들

Things to Know about Paintings

p.10~11

미술품이란 정확히 무엇일까? 그것은 어떤 소묘나 채색한 그림일까? 물론 그렇지 않고, 거기에는 조각품, 사진, 직물, 도자기를 포함하여 많은 다른 형태의 미술품이 있다.

현대 미술품이 런던의 테이트 모던 미술관에 전시되어 있다. 수년에 걸쳐, 거기에는 벽돌 더미, 거대한 미끄럼틀들, 그리고 수백만 개의 도자기 해바라기 씨로 가득 찬 홀이 포함되어 있다! TV 시리즈 〈심슨 가족〉의 어느 회차에서는 호머가 고철로 숯불구이용 그릴을 만들려다가 실패하고 만다. 그런데 그것이 현대 미술품으로 오인되어 대중들이 보도록 전시된다.

p.12~13

어떤 현대 미술품은 설치의 형태로 되어 있는데, 그것은 단지 짧은 시간 동안만 벌어지는 공연의 한 유형이다. 2016년 7월 9일에 스펜서 터닉이란 예술가가 영국의 해안 도시 헐에서 설치 미술 작품 하나를 만

들었다. 〈헐의 바다〉라고 하는 그 설치 미술품은 다른 색조의 푸른색으로 칠해진 3,200명의 벌거벗은 사람들로 이루어졌다! 터닉은 그 도시를 대표하는 곳들 앞에서 그 사람들의 사진을 찍었다. 그들은 건물들 주변으로 밀려들고 솟아오르는 바닷물을 나타냈다.

모든 연령층의 사람이 미술품을 창작하는 것을 즐긴다. 어릴 때부터 아이들은 색깔에 끌린다. 이것이 이 연령대에게 팔리는 책들이 총천연색 그림들로 그려지는 이유이다. 심지어 아주 어린 아이들조차 뭔가를 끄적거리고 표시하려 하는데, 항상 종이 위에만 그러는 게 아니다. 벽, 장난감, 가구, 그리고 심지어는 사람들까지도 그 위에 그림을 그리는 데 사용될 수 있다! 그렇지만 미국인 화가 아키아나 크라마리크처럼 재능 있는 아이들이 그렇게 많은 것은 아니다. 그녀는 여섯 살 때 기량이 뛰어난 성인 화가의 그림들 같은 믿기 어려운 그림들을 그리기 시작했다. 열두 살 즈음에는 60개의 작품을 완성했으며, 그 중 몇몇 개는 수천 달러에 팔렸다.

p.14~15

어떤 이들은 심지어 동물들도 미술 작품들을 창작한다고 믿는다. 오스트레일리아에서 수컷 새틴바우어새들은 암컷들을 유혹하기 위해 파란색 물건들을 모아 '정자'라는 구조물들로 그것들을 늘어놓는다. 꽃, 유리 조각, 음료 빨대, 그리고 빨래집게들이 모두 그 새들이 정성 들여 지은 정자들에서 발견되었다. 미

국 세인트루이스 동물원의 사육사들은 자신들이 보살피는 몇몇 동물들이 물감으로 실험하는 것을 허락하고 있다. 뱀, 유인원, 펭귄, 그리고 심지어는 곤충들까지도 캔버스에 물감 자국을 만들어낼 수 있다. 그들의 미술품들은 그 동물원이 펼치는 사업들의 기금을 마련하기 위해 판매된다.

모든 문화의 사람들은 미술품을 만들어내고, 그것은 역사에 대  해 알게 되는 중요한 방법이다. 동굴 그림들은 장장 4만 년 전인 선사시대 때부터 시작된다. 그것들은 대부분의 대륙에서 발견될 수 있다. 그것들은 손가락이나 간단한 도구들을 사용하여 동굴 벽에 그려졌다. 물감, 즉 안료는 흙과 돌멩이를 이용하여 만들어졌다. 그렇기 때문에 대부분의 동굴 벽화들은 빨간색, 검은색, 갈색, 또는 누르스름한 색이다. 2013년 영화 〈크루즈 가족〉에서는 한 원시인이 자신의 가족 이야기를 전하기 위해 동굴 벽에 그림들을 그린다. 아마도 그것들은 근처에 어떤 동물들이 살고, 어떻게 그것들을 잡는지에 대한 정보를 전달하는 방법이기도 했을 것이다.

p.16~17

 일부 문화권에서는 사람들이 문신의 형태로 자신들의 몸에 예술 작품을 만든다. 여러분은 재클린 윌슨의 어린이들을 위한 소설 〈문신 투성이 엄마〉에서 이렇게 했던 여인에 대해 읽을 수 있다. 종종 사람들은 그 모양새를 좋아해서 그것을 한다. 그러나 남태평양의 섬나라들과 같은 문화권에서는 이러한 문신으로 새겨진 상징들이 중요한 의미를 갖는다. 그것들은 어떤 사람이 어느 집안이나 부족에 속하는지를 보여줄 수 있다. 그것들은 종교적 혹은 영적인 믿음을 표현하기 위해 사용될 수도 있다.

사람들은 또 어떤 이유로 미술품을 창작할까? 어떤 사람들은 여느 다른 직업처럼 돈을 벌기 위해 그것을 한다. 사진이 존재하기 전, 화가들은 사람들이 어

떻게 생겼는지를 보여주기 위해  그들의 초상화를 그렸다. 1539년에 헨리 8세가 영국의 왕위에 있었을 때, 그는 화가 한스 홀바인을 독일로 보냈다. 홀바인의 임무는 클레베의 앤이라는 젊은 여성의 그림을 그리는 것이었다. 헨리는 그녀와의 결혼을 고려하고 있었으며, 그녀가 어떻게 생겼는지 보고 싶었다. 이것이 헨리에게 그녀의 생김새를 보여줄 수 있는 유일한 방식이었다.

p.18~19

 홀바인은 호감이 가는 초상화를 만들어냈고, 그래서 헨리는 그녀와 결혼하는 데 동의했다. 그런데 그가 실제로 앤을 봤을 때, 그는 그녀가 살찐 말처럼 생겼다고 말했다! 당연히, 홀바인은 두 번 다시 그 왕을 위해 그림을 그리라는 요청을 받지 않았다. 현대에는 사진작가들이 돈을 벌기 위해 사람들, 가족, 그리고 심지어 애완동물들 사진까지 촬영한다. 일부 유명한 화가들의 그림은 수백만 달러에 팔릴 수 있지만, 안타깝게도 많은 작가가 세상을 떠난 후에야 비로소 유명해진다.

많은 사람이 그저 그것을 즐기거나 뭔가 새로운 것을 배우고 싶기 때문에 미술품을 창작한다. 그들은 기량과 이해를 발달시킬 수 있다. 어쩌면 그들은 자연의 아름다움을 포착하거나 그들의 상상 속에 있는 무언가를 드러내려고 노력하고 싶은 것인지도 모  른다. 어쩌면 기쁨, 노여움, 또는 슬픔 같은 감정을 표현하고 싶은 것일 수도 있다.

p.20~21

다른 사람들은 어떤 메시지를 전달하고 싶기 때문에

예술품을 창작하기도 한다. 그들은 일어났던 일을 이야기하고 싶거나, 미래에 일어날 수도 있는 일에 대해 사람들에게 경고하고 싶어 한다. 예를 들면, 파블로 피카소의 유명한 그림 〈게르니카〉는 게르니카라는 스페인 마을이 폭격당한 후에 그려졌다. 그것

은 그 마을 사람들의 고통을 기록하고 있다. 그것은 또한 전쟁이 나쁜 것이란 메시지를 모든 사람에게 전하고 있다.

미술품은 그 미술품을 보는 사람들 역시 깊은 생각과 감정을 경험할 수 있게 하는 방식으로 그것들을 함께 나누는 하나의 방법이다. 그것은 사람들을 함께 모아 그들이 혼자가 아니라는 사실을 깨닫게 해주는 하나의 방식인 것이다. 따라서 미술품은 기본적으로 한 사람에게서 다른 사람에게로의 의사소통에 관한 것이다. 함께 나누고 싶은 어떤 감정이나 메시지를 가진 화가를 상상해 보자. 또한, 그 예술품을 보고 그 메시지를 전달받는 어떤 관람자를 마음속에 그려보자. 그 메시지는 어떻게 한 사람에게서 다른 이에게로 전해질까? 그것이 전달되는 것에 어떤 다른 사람들이 관련되어 있을까? 그 그림들의 여정을 처음부터 끝까지 살펴보기로 하자.

p.24~25

화가는 무엇을 그릴지 어떻게 결정할까? 화가들은 모든 종류의 다양한 장소에서 영감을 얻는다. 대다수 화가는 아이디어들이 어디에서든, 그리고 그들이 거의 예상하지 못한 뜻밖

의 순간에 떠오를 수 있다는 사실에 동의할 것이다! 어떤 화가들은 실제 대상을 그리는데, 그것은 자연적인 것이거나 인간이 만든 것일 수 있다. 이것은 '정물'화라고 불린다. 그 화가는 오래 지속되지 않을 무언가의 실제 모습을 포착하려 한다.

p.26~27

그렇기 때문에 사진이 대중화되기 이전의 과거에는 꽃들과 과일이 정물화의 인기 있는 선택이었으며, 오늘날에도 여전히 인기 있는 선택이다. 다른 화가들은 〈버터 더미〉라는 이 그림처럼 좀 더 특이한 대상들을 선택한다. 이것은 19세기에 프랑스 화가 앙트안느 발롱에 의해 그려졌다. 많은 화가들은 개개의 동물이나 식물을 그리기로 하든, 또는 풍경을 그리기로 하든, 자연에 영감을 받는다. 식물화가 마틴 J. 앨런은 아주 세밀한 식물화를 그린다. 그는 꽃봉오리가 열리기 시작하는 순간에 영감을 받는다. 변화의 순간을 포착한다는 이러한 발상은 1987년에 전시되었던 모든 그림에 영감을 주었다.

어떤 화가들은 자신들의 꿈에 의해 영감을 받는다. 오딜롱 르동이라는 프랑스 화가는 자칭 '검은' 그림들이라고 하는 것들을 그렸는데, 그것들은 그의 꿈과 악몽에서 나왔던 형상들로 이루어졌다. 1878년에 그는 〈물의 수호 정령〉을 그렸고, 거기에는 바다 위를 맴도는 얼굴이 담겨 있다.

p.28~29

다른 화가들, 특히 추상적인 작품(명확한 모습이 없는 패턴, 모양, 선들)을 그리는 사람들은 그냥 뭔가를 계속해 나가면서 아이디어를 얻는다고 주장한다. 그들은 어떤 느낌, 특별한 색을 사용하려는 욕구로부

터 시작하고, 이어서 그것이 어떻게 전개되는지를 본다. 아이디어가 어디에서 오는지에는 정말이지 아무런 한계가 없다. 그렇지만 일단 그 화가가 강렬한 창작 욕구를 가지게 되면, 그 여정은 시작될 수 있다.

일단 화가가 어떤 형상을 창작하고 싶은지 결정했다면, 다음 결정은 표현 수단들의 선택이다. 화가는 어디에 소묘나 그림을 그릴지, 그리고 무엇으로 소묘나 그림을 그릴지를 선택해야 한다. 화가는 거의 모든 것 위에 그림을 그릴 수 있다. 돌, 나무껍질, 나무, 도자기, 유리, 콘크리트, 가죽, 또는 심지어 사람 몸까지도 표현 수단의 어떤 대체 선택물이 될 수 있다. 이러한 소재들 하나하나는 저마다 물감을 칠하기가 얼마나 쉬운지, 또는 어려운지에 영향을 줄 수 있는 다른 특성들을 가지고 있다. 또한, 그것들은 물감이 얼마나 오랫동안 그 색깔과 겉모습을 유지할 것인지에 영향을 준다. 화가는 완성된 작품이 어떻게 보일지, 또는 어떤 메시지가 전달될지에 따라 그 표현 수단을 선택한다. 예를 들어, 어떤 화가는 사람들이 그림을 손으로 집어서 들고 있을 수 있도록 돌에 그림을 그리기로 선택할 수 있다. 그 돌이 *느껴지는* 방식이 그것이 *보이는* 방식만큼 중요할 수 있는 것이다.

p.30~31

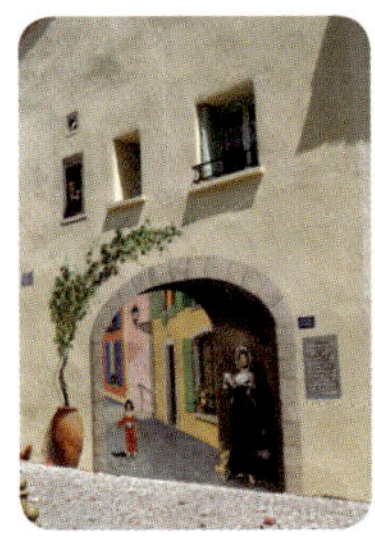

벽화는 안쪽이든 바깥쪽이든, 건물의 벽에 직접 그려지는 그림이다. 벽화는 빈민가로 변한 대도시 중심부 지역이나 삭막한 벽들에 활기를 주기 위해 이용될 수 있다. 일부 거리 화가들은 자신들의 작품이 만들어지자마자 대중들이 그것을 볼 수 있도록 보도 위에 직접 그린다. '트롱프뢰유'라는 독특한 유형의 벽화 또는 거리

예술이 있다. 이것은 '눈의 실수'라는 프랑스어이다. 이것은 착각이나 속임수를 만들어내는 예술품이다. 벽이나 보도에 구멍이 있는 것처럼 보이고, 보는 사람은 그 너머의 전혀 다른 무언가를 보는 것이다.

p.32~33

특히 세계적으로 유명한 그라피티 예술가 뱅크시에 의해 그려진다면 그라피티는 미술의 하나의 형식이 될 수 있는데, 그는 영국 출신이지만 전 세계에서 작업하고 있다. 뱅크시의 정체를 아는 사람은 아무도 없지만 그의 작품들은 잘 알려져 있다. 런던의 벽과 건물들에는 뱅크시의 예술품들이 많이 있다. 그것들 중 다수는 보호를 위해 퍼스펙스라는 투명 플라스틱으로 덮여 있다. 그러나 얼마 후에 그것들 중 일부는 페인트가 덧칠되거나, 그것들이 그려져 있는 벽이 제거된다. 그라피티 예술은 좀처럼 오랫동안 남아 있지 않지만, 소장을 위해 그 그림들의 사진이나 복사본을 구입할 수는 있다.

많은 화가들이 평평한 표면에 그림 그리기를 선택하는데, 그것은 나중에 감상을 위해 벽에 걸릴 수 있다. 과거에 화가들은 이를 위해 주로 나무를 사용했다. 1503년에 그려진 레오나르도 다빈치의 유명한 〈모나리자〉는 포플러 나무에 그려졌다. 현대 화가들은 보통 종이나 캔버스를 선택한다. 또한, 지금의 그 선택은 화가가 무엇으로 그림을 그리고 싶은지에 달려 있기도 하다. 물감에는 여러 종류가 있으며, 그것들은 다른 유형의 표면을 필요로 한다.

p.34~35

세 가지 주된 종류의 물감은 유화 물감, 수채화 물감, 아크릴 물감이다. 유화 물감은 튜브에 들어 있으며, 대개 캔버스 천으로 만들어진 표면에 칠해진다.

이것은 그림뿐만 아니라 돛과 텐트에 사용되는 질기고 촘촘하게 짜인 직물이다. 그것은 찢기가 어렵다. 수채화 물감은 종종 주석 통에 들어 있는 단단한 사각형 안료들이다. 그렇지 않으면, 튜브에 들어 있는 것으로 구입되어, 팔레트 위에 짜내서 굳어지게 둘 수도 있다. 그것들은 보통 종이 위에 칠해진다. 그것들을 사용하려면 화가는 그림 붓에 약간의 물을 묻혀 단단한 물감의 표면을 적신다. 이렇게 하면 종이 위에 칠해졌을 때 강렬하고 밝은색이 된다. 물을 더 묻히면 묻힐수록, 물감은 더 옅어지고, 그러면 화가는 옅은, 거의 투명한 '얇은 층'을 만들어낼 수 있다.

p.36~37

1800년대 초에 창작된 윌리엄 베리먼의 이 수채화는 그가 먼저 그림을 스케치하고 나서 수채화 물감으로 그것을 채워 넣기 시작한 방식을 보여준다. 이것은 자메이카에서 그려졌고, 〈자메이카 오두막〉이라는 단순한 제목을 갖고 있다. 그러나 이 그림은 마무리되지 못했고, 따라서 완성되었다면 아마도 베리먼이 다른 제목을 붙였을지도 모른다. 만약 이것이 여러분의 그림이었다면 어떤 제목을 붙이겠는가?

유화 물감과 수채화 물감 이외에, 현대 화가가 고를 수 있는 세 번째 선택인 아크릴 물감이 있

다. 아크릴 물감은 20세기에 발명되었다. 그것은 여러 다양한 표면에 많은 다양한 방식으로 사용될 수 있다. 아크릴 물감은 더 옅게 만들기 위해 수채화 물

감처럼 물과 섞을 수 있고, 또는 짙고 끈적끈적한 형태로 튜브에 들어 있는 것에서 곧바로 사용될 수도 있다. 아크릴 물감은 물을 이용해서 옷이나 피부에서 씻겨나가기 때문에 만약 그게 아직 젖은 상태라면 닦기가 쉽다. 만약 물감이 말랐다면 좀 더 어렵긴 하지만 매니큐어 제거제로 제거될 수 있다. 유화 물감은 제거하기가 훨씬 더 어렵다. 그래서 아크릴 물감은 그림을 그리는 동안 마구 어지럽혀 놓는 사람들에게 좋다!

p.38~39

유화 물감과 아크릴 물감은 거칠거칠한 질감을 가진 그림을 그리기에 좋다. 이것은 붓이나 팔레트 나이프라는 이름의 납작한 칼로 물감을 두껍게 찍어 바르면 된다. 이것은 1889년에 그려진 빈센트 반 고흐의 유화 〈별이 빛나는 밤〉에서 확실하

게 볼 수 있다. 물감의 거칠거칠한 질감은 마치 별들이 움직이고, 빛나고 있는 것처럼 보이게 해 준다.

3장. 그림 그리기

p.42~43

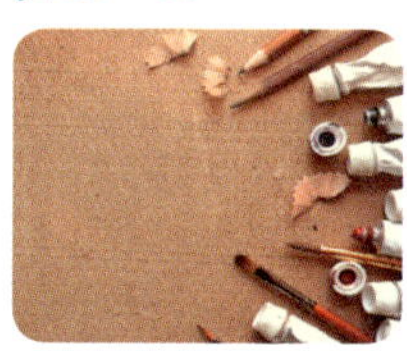

일단 화가가 무엇을 그릴 것인지, 그리고 어떤 표현 도구들을 쓸 것인지 결정하면, 이젠 *어디에서* 그림 작업을 할지 결정할 시간이다. 풍경화를 그리고 싶은 화가는 밖으로 나가는 쪽을 택할지도 모른다. 그 사람은 자신이 그리고 싶은 경치 앞에 앉거나 설 수 있다. 만약 그것이 여러 날 동안에 걸쳐 변할 것 같지 않은 경관이라면, 그리고 날씨가 계속 알맞은 상태로 있다면, 화가는 전체 그림을 밖에서 완성할 수도 있다.

대개 그 사람은 먼저 연필 스케치를 하고, 정확한 색

조가 요구되는 곳에 섞어 둔 물감을 약간 칠할 수도 있다. 화가는 그 경치가 정확히 어떤 모습인지 기억하기 위해 사진들을 찍고 그 스케치에 메모를 써넣을 수도 있다. 그런 다음, 화가는  실제 그림을 그려내기 위해 실내로 들어간다. 때때로, 어떤 화가는 전적으로 사진 한 장을 가지고 작업을 한다. 이것은 대상이 완전히 변함없는 상태로 유지된다는 사실과 같은 여러 가지 이점이 있다. 만약 어떤 화가가 사람이나 동물을 그리고 있다면, 사진을 모사하는 것이 더 쉬울 수 있다. 그 대상은 움직이거나, 불평하거나, 하루하루 외양을 바꾸지 않는 것이다! 그렇지만, 어떤 화가들은 원래 대상, 즉 실제 사람이나 동물로 작업하는 것을 선호한다. 그들은 자신들의 그림이 그 대상의 외양뿐만 아니라 특성도 포착하기를 원하는 것이다.

p.44~45

많은 화가들은 실내에서 그림 그리기를 택한다. 일부 화가들은 자기 집의 평범한 방을 사용한다. 이러려면 신중한 생각이 요구되는데, 그냥 아무 방이나 되는 것이 아니기 때문이다. 만약 어떤 화가가 커다란 그림을 그릴 예정이라면, 그것은 이젤 위에 세워질 수도 있는데, 그건 많은 공간을 차지한다. 치워야 할 많은 쓰레기가 있을 수 있고, 방에 온  통 스케치나 사진들이 핀으로 부착될 수도 있다. 그 화가는 이러한 것들을 매일 깔끔히 정리해야 하는 쪽보다는 그대로 내버려 둘 수 있는 장소가 필요하다.

그 방은 많은 자연광이 필요하고, 따라서 커다란 창문들이 도움이 된다. 그  러나 빛은 온종일 변한다. 아침에 따뜻한 햇볕을 많이 받는 방은 오후

동안에는 좀 더 어둡고 침침할 수 있다. 빛의 변화는 대상의 색채 변화를 일으키고, 그림자를 드리울 수도 있다. 이런 이유로 북반구에 있는 어떤 화가들은 북향의 방을 고른다. 그곳은 햇살을 덜 받지만, 그 빛은 온종일 거의 일정하다.

p.46~47

어떤 화가들은 오롯이 자신들의 예술을 위해서만 확보된, 작업실이라고 하는 방을 가질 만큼 운이 좋  다. 그들은 작업실로 들어가서는 주의를 산만하게 만드는 생활의 모든 것들에서 벗어나 자신들의 그림에 집중할 수 있다. 그렇다면, 화가의 작업실은 어떤 모습이어야 할까? 레오나르도 다빈치는 작업실은 화가가 집중하는 것을 돕기 위해 작아야 한다고 말했다. 모든 사람이 동의하는 것은 아니다. 파블로 피카소는 자신의 많은 작품이 보관되었던 아주 넓은 작업실을 가졌다. 또한 그는 모델과 방문객들도 접대했다.

 어떤 화가들은 그림들이 크기 때문에 커다란 작업실이 필요하다. 1956년에 세상을 떠난 미국 화가 잭슨 폴록은 바닥에 캔버스들을 놓고 그것들 위에 물감을 방울방울 떨어뜨리거나 끼얹어 거대한 그림들을 만들어냈다. 작업실은 그저 그림만을 위한 곳이 아닐 수도 있다. 만약 어떤 화가가 뭔가 작업을 하면서 여러 시간을 보낼 예정이라면, 거기에는 흔히 작은 주방, 소파, 또는 심지어 침대까지도 있다. 어떤 화가들은 작업실이 말끔해야만 작업할 수 있다. 그러나 또 어떤 화가들은 창작하기에 너무 바쁜 나머지 자기 주변의 난장판을 알아차리지도 못한다.

p.48~49

아일랜드의 더블린을 여행하는 사람들은 1992년

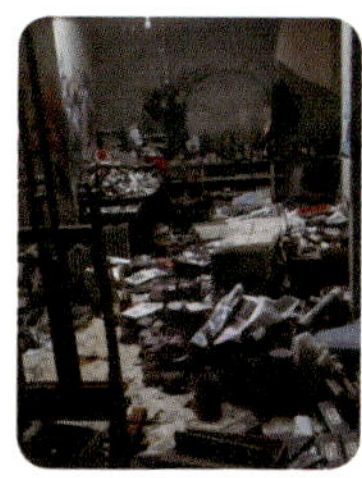

에 세상을 떠난 아일랜드 태생 화가인 프랜시스 베이컨 소유의 작업실 모형관을 방문할 수 있다. 그 바닥은 물감의 주석 통들, 사진들, 신문에서 오려낸 기사들, 그리고 온갖 종류의 물체들로 뒤덮여 있다. 언젠가 프랜시스 베이컨은 너무 깔끔하게 정돈된 장소들에서는 작업할 수 없다는 말을 했었다. 그는 지저분한 작업실에서 그림을 그리는 것이 훨씬 더 쉽다는 것을 발견했다.

일단 화가가 시작할 준비가 되면, 어떤 색깔들을 사용할지 선택해야 한다. 물감 색깔은 그것이 유화 물감이든 수채화 물감 혹은 아크릴 물감이든, 재미난 이름들을 가진 많은 다양한 색조로 생산된다. 전문 화가가 소장하는 물감에는 단순하게 '파란색'이 들어 있지 않을 것이다. 거기에는 '울트라마린', '코발트 블루'와 '프러시안 블루' 같은 흥미진진한 이름들이 포함되어 있을 수 있다. 물론, 화가는 물감들을 섞어 무엇이든 자신이 원하는 색상을 만들어낼 수 있다. 흰색을 추가하면 색깔이 더 옅어질 것이다. 검은색을 아주 조금 추가하면 색이 더 어두워질 것이다. 원색인 빨강색, 파랑색, 그리고 노랑색을 다른 조합으로 섞으면, 자주색, 주황색, 그리고 초록색 색조가 나올 것이다. 몇몇 현대 미술 화가들은 오로지 한 가지 색깔에만 집중한다. 그들은 특별히 아름답거나 강렬한 그 색의 새로운 색조를 만들어내는 것을 목표로 한다.

p.50~51

그림을 그리는 과정은 화가 개개인이 다르다. 어떤 화가들은 그림의 아주 작은 부분을 완벽하게 하려고 시간을 보낸다. 또 어떤 화가들은 전체 그림의 대략적인 아이디어를 만들어놓은 다음에 그것의 부분들을 바꾼다. 그들은 색깔을 추가하거나 바꾸고, 실수를 바로잡는다. 어떤 사람들은 일단 그림이 다 끝나면 고칠 수 없다고 생각하지만, 이것은 사실이 아니다. 미술사가들은 화가가 그림을 그리는 동안에 그 그림에 대한 생각을 바꿨다는 것을 암시하는 그림들에 '펜티멘토'라는 용어를 사용한다. 이따금 이것은 전문가들에 의해 관찰될 수 있는데, 그들은 완성된 그림과 어울리지 않는 듯한 물감 흔적들이 있다는 사실을 알아차린다. 흔히, 원화의 이런 흔적들은 그 그림을 살펴보기 위해 엑스레이나 적외선 기술을 사용하기 전에는 눈에 보이지 않는다.

p.52~53

이것의 좋은 예는 〈아르놀피니 부부의 초상〉이다. 그것은 1434년에 얀 반 에이크가 그렸다. 그 초상화에 대한 과학적 검사로 얀 반 에이크가 바꾼 부분들이 드러났다. 눈, 손, 그리고 발이 원래는 다른 위치에 있었다. 이러한 변경은 대부분 그 그림이 단지 '밑그림'일 때 이루어졌다. 이것은 물감을 칠하기 전에 바꿨다는 의미가 된다. 그러나 몇몇 변경은 색을 입히는 바로 그 과정 동안에 행해졌다.

어떤 것들은 다른 것들보다 바꾸기가 더 쉽다. 화가는 아크릴 물감을 썼을 때, 원화의 물감을 가능한 한 많이 제거할 수 있다. 그런 다음, 그 부분에는 티탄백 물감을 칠할 수 있다. 이렇게 하면 새로운 색깔을 덧칠할 수 있는 하얀 바탕이 생긴다. 유화 물감으로는 그렇게 하는 것이 그 정도로 쉽지 않다. 물감을 여러 겹 덧칠하면 그야말로 실수에 더 큰 관심을 끌게할 수도 있다. 그러나 아직 마르지 않은 유화 물감은 부드러운 천을 사용하여 지울 수 있다. 마지막 흔적들을 지우기 위해서는 약간의 아마인유를 추가할 수도 있다. 수채화 물감은 물에 용해되기 때문에 물을 더 추가하여 다시 적실 수 있다. 그런 다음, 흡수력 있는 종이 키친타월로 제거할 수 있다. 일단 물감을 칠한 표면이 다시 마르면, 화가는 새로운 물감으로 그림을 계속 그릴 수 있다.

p.56~57

드디어 그림이 완성되었다! 이제는 그 그림이 더 멀리 여행하기 위해서는 다른 직업들을 가진 더 많은 사람들이 필요해진다. 다음 단계는 대체로 액자에 넣는 일이다. 이 작업은 화가가 그 방법을 알고 있으면 스스로 할 수도 있지만, 흔히 그림 액자 작업자가 한다. 완성된 그림을 액자에 넣는 주된 이유는 두 가지이다. 첫째는 그림을 멋지게 보이도록 하기 위해서이다. 둘째는 손상으로부터 그것을 보호하기 위한 것이다.

대부분의 그림은 액자에 넣어져 전시되지만, 몇몇 현대의 캔버스들은 액자 없이 전시되기

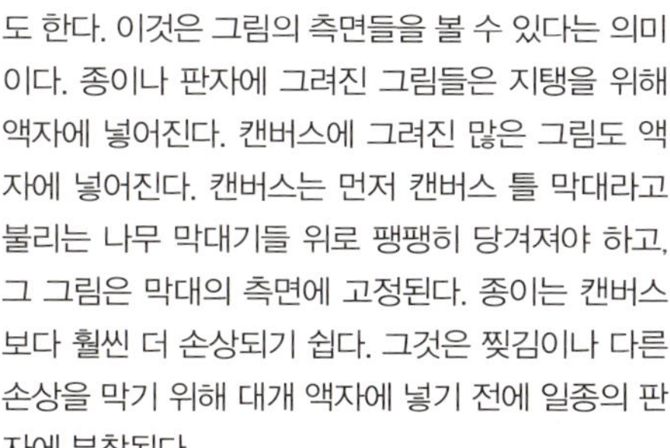

도 한다. 이것은 그림의 측면들을 볼 수 있다는 의미이다. 종이나 판자에 그려진 그림들은 지탱을 위해 액자에 넣어진다. 캔버스에 그려진 많은 그림도 액자에 넣어진다. 캔버스는 먼저 캔버스 틀 막대라고 불리는 나무 막대기들 위로 팽팽히 당겨져야 하고, 그 그림은 막대의 측면에 고정된다. 종이는 캔버스보다 훨씬 더 손상되기 쉽다. 그것은 찢김이나 다른 손상을 막기 위해 대개 액자에 넣기 전에 일종의 판자에 부착된다.

p.58~59

보통, 그림은 특히 종이에 그려졌으면, 유리를 덮은 액자에 넣어진다. 유리는 공기 중의 먼지나 화학물질들로부터 그 그림을 보호하여 좋은 상태로 유지시킨다. 그것은 사람들이 그 그림을 만지지 못하게 막는다. 그것은 또 그 그림에 도달하는 빛, 특히 자외선의 양을 감소시키기도 한다. 비록 그 그림을 보고 그것의 색채를 감상하기 위해서는 빛이 필요하지만, 과도한 빛은 그림을 손상시킬 수 있다. 그래서 많은 미술관이 조명을 희미하게 밝히는 것이다.

유화는 그것들을 보호하기 위해 유리가 필요하지 않다. 대신, 그 그림 위에 투명한 니스를 한 겹 덧칠한다. 이 부분에서 화가는 매우 인내심이 있어야 한다. 유화는 완성된 지 6개월 후에나 니스칠이 되어야만 하는 것이다! 이것은 물감이 반드시 완전히 마르도록 하기 위해서이다. 만약 물감이 아주 두껍다면, 화가는 훨씬 더 오래 기다려야 한다. 니스를 너무 일찍 덧칠하면, 물감이 마르기 전에 니스가 마르게 될 것이다. 얼마 후에 표면에 균열들이 나타날 것이다. 그 그림은 값어치가 없어질 테고, 화가는 그것으로 돈을 벌기가 어렵다는 것을 알게 될 것이다. 간혹, 특별히 박물관과 미술관들에 있는 유화들은 유리가 덮인 액자에 넣어진

다. 이것은 보통 일반인들에 의해 손상될 수 있는 매우 귀중한 그림들을 보호하기 위한 것이다.

p.60~61

다음 결정 사항은 사용할 액자의 종류이다. 어떤 액자들은 매우 가늘고 소박하다. 또 어떤 액자들은 아주 정교하며, 조각되거나 틀에 넣어져 화려한 형태로 만들어진다. 액자는 전통적으로는 나무로 만들어지지만, 현대에는 금속이나 특정한 플라스틱으로 만들어질 수도 있다. 어떤 액자들은 '금박이 입혀지기'도 한다. 이 말은 그것들이 마치 금으로 되어 있는 것처럼 보이게끔 만들어진다는 의미이다. 이것은 액자들에 금색 페인트를 칠하거나 금박을 입히면 가능할 수 있다. 금박은 고운 붓으로 조금씩 덧칠되는, 극도로 얇은 순금 막이다.

액자 작업이 완료되면, 그 그림은 전시되고 판매용으로 내놓을 채비가 갖춰진 것이다. 이 시점에서, 화가는 여러 사람의 도움이 필요할 수 있  다. 그들은 화가의 그림 판매를 돕고, 가장 광범위한 관람객들에게 도달할 수 있게 도울 수 있다. 물론, 화가들이 직접 자신의 작품을 팔 수도 있다. 그러나 그 것에는 더 많은 그림을 그리는 데 쓰일 수도 있을 많은 시간과 노력이 들어간다. 이런 이유로 많은 화가들은 중개인의 도움을 이용하는 쪽을 택한다. 미술 중개인은 화가들의 작품이 적절한 장소에 전시되고 적합한 사람들에게 팔리도록 화가들을 대신해서 일하는 사람이다. 중개인은 대개 예술계에서 오랜 경험을 가진 사람이다. 중개인은 구매자, 미술관, 그리고 경매 회사들(이것에 대해서는 다음 장에서 다룰 것이다)과 많은 연줄이 있다.

p.62~63

중개인은 화가가 버는 돈의 일부 비율을 취함으로써 이익을 얻는다. 이 것은 '수수료'를 위 해 일하는 것이라고 불린다. 이 말은 화가가 돈을 많이 벌면 벌수록, 중개상도 더 많은 돈을 번다는 의미이다! 어떤 중개인들은 화가를 위하여 일하는 대신 미술관을 위해 일한다. 그들은 전시하고 판매할 적절한 예술품들을 찾아 돌아다닌다. 그들은 현재 전시할 준비가 된 작품이 있는지 물어보기 위해 화가들을 접촉할 수도 있다. 이런 방식으로 일하는 많은 중개인들은 특정 양식의 미술품에 관한 전문가들이다. 그들은 새롭고 마음 설레게 하는 화가들을 찾기 위하여 전 세계를 자주 여행한다.

이미 꽤 유명하고 성공한 화가들은 아트 매니저의 도움을 이용할 수도 있다. 팝 스타 같은 많은 음악가들은 그들의 직업상 모든 일을 처리하기 위해 매니저를 이용한다. 아트 매니저는 화가를 위해 비슷한 일을 한다. 그 매니저는 화가의 모든 업무를 돌본다.

금전 관리, 마케팅, 그리고 홍보 행사들이 매니저가 처리할 수 있는 몇몇 업무이다. 물론, 그림 그리는 일로 경력을 막 시작하고 있는 화가라면 중개인이 없을 수 있고, 매니저는 분명히 없을 것이다. 그 화가는 그림 보는 것을 즐기고, 심지어는 구입하고 싶어 할 만한 사람들 앞에 자기 그림들을 가져다 놓을 필요가 있다. 이렇게 하기 위한 최상의 방법은 미술관에서 전시회를 여는 것이다.

p.66~67

미술관은 그림과 같은 예술품을 전시할 공간을 많이 가진 방이나 건물이다. 그것들은 관람자들이 와서 그림을 감상할 수 있도록 개방된다. 심지어 허구의 첩보원 제임스 본드조차 미술관을 찾아간다! 2012년 영화 〈007 스카이폴〉에서 제임스 본드는 그의 상관 Q를 런던의 국립 미술관에서 만난다.

〈진주 귀고리를 한 소녀〉라 는 유명한 그림을 훔치는 아 주 불량한 여학생들에 관한 2007년 영화 〈세인트 트리니 안스〉에도 같은 미술관이 등 장한다. 이곳은 공립 미술관이 며, 작품이 판매되지 않는 곳  이다. 좀 더 작은 미술관들은 특별 행사나 전시회를 개최하는데, 그곳에서는 특정 화가의 작품이 전시되고 판매될 수도 있다. 대개, 전시회 첫날밤에는 특별한 행사가 있다. 해당 화가는 그림들을 구입할 수도 있는 초대 손님들과 함께 참석한다. 보통 음식물이 제공되며, 재미난 사교 행사이다.

p.68~69

만약 어떤 화가가 미술관에서 작품을 전시한다면, 바라건대 사람들이 와서 작품을 구입할 것이다. 특히 가격이 높으면, 때때로 그들은 곧바로 작품을 구입하지 않는다. 그 화가는 카탈로그가 필요하다. 이것은 그림들의 사진과 가격에 대한 세부 정보가 실린 화려한 잡지 형태의 책자이다. 고객들은 이 카탈로그들을 가져가 시간을 두고 결정을 내린다. 일부 고객들은 단순히 어떤 그림을 보는 것이 좋고, 그것이 집에 걸려 있는 것이 보고 싶어서 구입하기를 원할 수 있다. 또 어떤 고객들은 미술품을 수집하고 그것을 투자로 보기 때문에 그림을 구입한다. 이 말은, 그들은 훗날에 훨씬 더 많은 돈의 가치가 있을 것으로 생각하는 그림만 구입한다는 의미이다. 그러한 고객들은 그 화가에 대해 더 많이 알아내는 일에 특히 관심을 가질 것이다. 그들은 그 화가와 작품 양쪽에 모두 투자해야 할지를 결정해야 하는 것이다. 이런 이유로, 그림으로 생계를 유지하는 것을 진지하게 생각하는 화가는 웹사이트를 가져야 한다. 여기에서, 그들은 자신과 작품들에 대한 정보를 줄 수 있다.

미술계에는 또 하나 중요한 일이 있는데, 그것은 고객들이 어떤 그림을 살지 말지 결정하는 것을 도와준다. 이것은 미술 비평가의 일이다. 미술 비평가는 미술품을 살펴보고 그것이 얼마나 잘 그려졌는지에 대해 생각하는 사람이다. 비평가들은 모든 종류의 예술품에 대해 의견을 제공한다. 그들은 잡지, 신문, 전시회 카탈로그, 그리고 웹사이트에 미술품에 대한 글을 쓴다. 고객들은 비평가들이 쓴 견해를 읽는다. 그들은 무엇을 구입할지에 대한 결정을 돕는 데 그 견해를 이용한다.

p.70~71

미술 비평가들의 이색적인 업무가 2016년에 처음으로 행해졌는데, 그때 몇몇 비평가는 제1회 연례 로봇 미술 경연대회에서 출품작들을 심사했다. 전

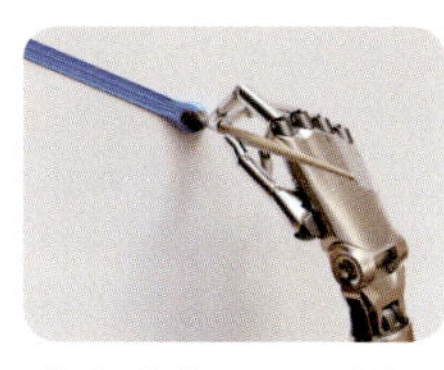

세계의 팀들에게 개방된 이 경연대회는 로봇이 만들어낸 예술품들에 10만 달러 상당의 상을 제공한다! 로봇들은 두 가지 방식으로 그림을 그릴 수 있다. 사람이 리모컨을 이용하여 로봇팔을 조작할 수도 있고, 또는 로봇이 컴퓨터 소프트웨어를 이용하여 조종될 수 있다. 가장 단순한 기법 중 하나는 로봇이 어떤 사진이나 그림을 베끼는 것이다. 그것은 한 번에 한 가지 색을 칠하며, 따라서 예를 들어 그림의 빨간 부분들이 전부 맨 먼저 칠해질 수 있다. 그다음에는 파란 부분들 전부, 노란 부분들, 그리고 등등. 이런 식으로, 그림이 서서히 만들어지는 것이다.

그림을 판매하는 또 하나의 방식은 미술품 '경매 회사'를 통해서이다. 경매 회사는 모든 종류의 물품을 판매한다. 미술관에서는 미술품의 가격이 정해져 있

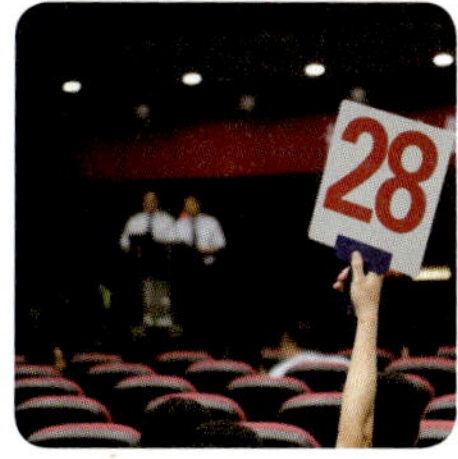

다. 경매는 다르다. 그것은 사람들이 얼마를 지불하고 싶은지를 결정하는 특이한 판매 유형이다. '경매사'라는 전문 판매자가 모인 사람들에게 그림을 보여준다. 경매사는 사람들이 얼마를 제시, 또는 '부르고' 싶은지 묻는다. 그 그림의 구입에 관심이 있는 사람들은 손을 들거나 고개를 끄덕인다. 이것은 자신이 다른 구매자들과 경쟁하고 싶다는 뜻을 경매사에게 전해 준다.

p.72~73

매번, 호가는 높아지고 그림 가격도 올라간다. 가격이 더 높아질수록, 일부 경매 참가자들은 경쟁에서 떨어져 나간다. 경매사는 단 두세 명의 경매 참가자가 남을 때까지 계속 호가를 묻는다. 마침내, 그 그림은 가장 높은 가격을 부른 사람에게 팔린다. 세계에서 가장 유명한 미술품 경매 회사 두 곳은 크리스티와 소더비이다. 그들은 여러분이 상상할 수 있는 모든 종류의 미술품을 판매한다. 이 두 경매 회사들은 모두 런던과 뉴욕에 유명한 경매장을 갖고, 전 세계

적으로 영업을 펼치고 있다. 2010년, 〈누드, 녹색 잎과 상반신〉이라는 파블로 피카소의 그림 한 점이 크리스티에 의해 매물로 나왔다. 그것은 8분 만에 1억 650만 달러라는 믿을 수 없는 액수에 팔렸다. 피카소는 이 그림을 단 하루에 그렸다. 그것은 하루 작업치고는 괜찮은 급료이다! 피카소는 세상을 떠날 때 부유했다. 그렇더라도 여전히 그 급료에 대해서는 깜짝 놀랐을 것이다.

p.74~75

그러나 경매 회사는 신진 화가들이 일반적으로 그림을 판매하는 장소는 아니다. 경매 회사에서 팔리는 그림 중 상당수는 유명한 작가들의 작품이다. 이따금, 고객들이 오랜 세월에 걸쳐 투자로 소장 그림들을 많이 모을 수 있다. 그런 다음, 돈을 벌기 위해 그 그림들의 일부 또는 전부를 경매 회사에서 팔 수 있다. 에스라와 데이비드 나마드라는 두 남자는 세계에서 가장 값나가는 미술 소장품을 소유하고 있다. 그것은 가치가 약 30억 달러로 평가된다! 그들의 소장품은 스위스 제네바 공항 인근의 창고에 보관되어 있다. 이것은 그들이 미술품을 감상하는 것이 좋아서 그것을 구입하는 것이 아니라는 점을 암시한다. 그러나 그들은 그것으로 많은 돈을 벌고 있으며, 뉴욕의 크리스티에서 가장 빈번하게 미술품을 판매하는 사람들이다.

또 한 사람의 대단한 미술품 수집가는 일라이 브로드라는 미국의 억만장자인데, 8,000점의 예술품을 소유하고 있다.

그는 이 작품들을 가능한 많은 사람들이 즐기기를 원하고 있으며, 따라서 그림들을 미술

관, 박물관, 대학교들에 대여하고 있다. 따라서, 미술품이 많은 다양한 이유로 창작되는 것과 마찬가지로, 또한 다양한 이유로 구매되기도 하는 것이다. 화가들은 그토록 열심히 작업한 그림이 사람들 눈에 띄지 않게 보관되고 오로지 돈을 벌기 위해서만 세상에 나오게 될 때 어떤 생각이 들까? 그것은 알기가 어려운데, 최고가로 팔리는 그림들 중 상당수는 오래전에 세상을 떠난 화가들 작품이기 때문이다. 다행히도, 그것들 가운데 많은 작품은 누구나 볼 수 있도록 공공 미술관에서 전시되고 있다.

p.76~77

공공 미술관에서 전시되고 있는 어떤 그림들은 수 세기가 된 것들이다. 그것들은 예술계의 몇몇 더 중요한 사람들의 관심을 필요로 한다. 이 사람들은 큐레이터와 보존 처리 전문가들이다. 미술 큐레이터의 업무는 일반 전시를 위해 미술 작품들을 한자리에 모으고 관리하는 일이다. 주요 공공 미술관의 큐레이터는 어떤 그림을 구입할지 결정한다. 또한 그 사람은 벽에 어떤 것들을 걸지, 어떤 것을 당분간 주의하여 보관할지, 그리고 어떤 것을 다른 미술관들에 대여할지도 결정한다. 큐레이터의 업무에는 그 그림들에 대해 세심한 기록을 계속하는 일도 포함된다. 또한, 그 업무에는 라벨 제작, 서면 정보와 카탈로그에 게재된 그림들의 소개 글 작성도 포함된다.

1997년에 나온 코미디 영화 〈빈〉에는 로스앤젤레스에 있는 한 미술관의 큐레이터가 등장하는데, 그의 이름은 데이비드 랭글리이다. 데이비드는 빈 씨가 런던의 국립 미술관에서 파견한 유명한 미술 비평가라고 믿는다. 그래서 그는 빈을 자기 집에서 머물도록 초대한다. 그러나 국립 미술

관에서는 그를 쫓아내기 위해 경비원인 빈 씨를 파견했을 뿐이었다. 빈 씨가 유명하고 값나가는 그림 〈휘슬러의 어머니〉를 뜻하지 않게 손상시키자 데이비드는 겁에 질린다. 그는 그 그림들을 제대로 관리할 책임이 있기 때문에 일자리를 잃을 수도 있다는 것을 알고 있다. 큐레이터가 된다는 것은 책임이 막중한 일인 것이다!

p.78~79

미술 작품 보존 처리 전문가의 일은 좀 더 기술적이다. 첫째, 그들은 미술품을 보존한다. 이 말은, 그들이 미술품을 피해나 손상으로부터 보호한다는 의미이다. 그들은 그것을 가능한 한 본래 상태에 가깝도록 유지하기 위해 노력한다. 또한 그들은 손상된 예술품을 보수하기도 한다. 그것들은 본래 상태로 복원, 즉 되살아나게 된다. 손상은 그동안의 세월, 또는 수분이나 빛 같은 환경 문제들에 의해 가해졌을 수 있다. 간혹, 어떤 그림의 복원이 실제로 더 많은 손상을 초래할지도 모른다. 비록 복원이 조심스럽게 행해지더라도, 사람들은 그 결과를 좋아하지 않을 수도 있다.

미술품 복원은 오직 전문가들에 의해서만 행해져야 한다. 사라고사라는 스페인의 작은 도시에는 벽화인 프레스코가 그려진 교회가 있다. 그 프레스코화는 예수의 그림이고, 수백 년이 된 것이다. 그 마을에 살던 여든 살 노파가 예수의 얼굴에 하얀 부분들이 생겼다는 것을 알아차리고는 직접 그것을 고치기로 결심했다. 그녀는 오래된 예수 얼굴 위에 새로운 얼굴을 그렸다. 안타깝게도, 새 얼굴은 전혀 딴판으로 보였다! 그러나 그것은 이제 인기 높은 관광 명소이다.

p.80~81

어떤 그림이 제대로 복원될 때, 거기에는 흔히 많은 과학이 연관된다. 레이저는 먼지를 제거하기 위해 사용될 수 있다. 그것은 표면층을 뜨겁게 만들어 팽창시킨다. 이렇게 하면, 표면에서 먼지를 들어 올리는 압력파가 생긴다. 레이저 광선은 짧은 시간, 대개 1초 이하로만 사용되지만, 매우 강력하다. 일부 미술품 복원가들은 그림을 닦기 위해 박테리아를 이용한다. 특정 박테리아는 효소라는 화학물질을 만들어낸다. 그 효소는 아무런 손상을 입히지 않고 먼지

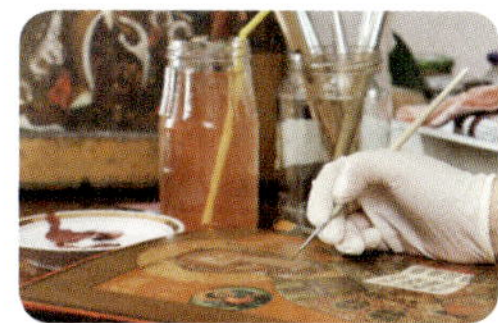

를 분해하여 그림 표면에서 들어 올린다.

이제 그림의 여행은 막을 내린다. 그것은 그려지고, 액자에 넣어지고, 팔리고, 전시되어 많은 사람들이 즐겁게 감상할 수 있다. 어떤 그림들을 감상하기 위해 미술관을 찾아가 보는 건 어떨까? 아니면, 직접 그림을 하나 그리고 액자에 넣어보는 건 어떨까? 다음에 어떤 그림을 볼 때는 그것을 만들어내기 위해 연관되었던 모든 사람들을 생각해 보자. 그렇지만 무엇보다도 그 작품을 즐기면서 바라보라. 그 화가가 주고 싶었던 메시지를 추측할 수 있을지 확인해

보라. 그 메시지는 여러분에게 도달하기 위해 먼 길을 여행해 온 것이다!

똑똑한 영어 읽기 **Wise & Wide**

독후 테스트

제목: Things to Know about Paintings

단계: Level 6

문항 구성: 어휘(7문항)

내용 이해(16문항)

문장 구조 · 문법(7문항)

❖ 독후 테스트는 홈페이지(www.darakwon.co.kr)에서 온라인으로도 풀어보실 수 있습니다.
이 경우 점수와 응시 결과에 대한 평가까지 확인하실 수 있습니다.
추가로 제공되는 단어 퀴즈도 풀어보세요.

1. What is an art "installation"?

① art that hangs on a wall

② art that is a performance

③ art that is made for people to wear

④ art that has no title

2. What does "hovering" mean in the following sentence?

Guardian Spirit of the Waters shows a face <u>hovering</u> over the sea.

① looking

② floating

③ threatening

④ guarding

3. What does "fragile" mean?

① white

② useful

③ delicate

④ cheap

※ Choose the right word for each blank. (4~5)

4.
관광객들은 프랜시스 베이컨 소유의 작업실의 모형관을 방문할 수 있다.

→ Tourists can go and visit a(n) ___________ of the studio belonging to Francis Bacon.

① replica

② structure

③ artwork

④ exhibition

5.

이따금, 고객들이 오랜 세월에 걸쳐 투자로써 소장 그림들을 많이 모을 수 있다.

→ Sometimes, customers may build up a collection of paintings over many years as a(n) ____________.

① communication
② commission
③ responsibility
④ investment

6. What is the common word for the two blanks?

If an artist is going to paint a large painting, it may be set ____________ on an easel, which takes ____________ a lot of space.

① on
② up
③ out
④ with

7. What are the proper words for the blanks?

• When the framing is complete, the painting is ready to be displayed and put ____________ for sale.
• The art curator's job is to create and care ____________ a collection of art for public display.

① to – of
② up – for
③ to – of
④ up – in

8. Why are most cave paintings painted using red, black, brown, or yellowish colors?
   ① People did not like other colors in those days.
   ② The colors were made using earth and rocks.
   ③ A wide range of colors were used, but time has changed them all to dull colors.
   ④ Green and blue colors were spoiled because people painted with dirty fingers.

9. What is recorded in the painting *Guernica*?
   ① the beauty of Spanish scenery
   ② the shape of Spanish buildings
   ③ the suffering of Spanish people
   ④ the variety of Spanish animals

10. What message did Picasso want to give people in his painting, *Guernica*?
   ① War is exciting.
   ② War is a bad thing.
   ③ War doesn't happen anymore.
   ④ War helps people to be brave.

11. What does a botanical artist paint?
   ① animals
   ② plants
   ③ insects
   ④ people

12. What type of art consists of patterns, shapes, and lines without an obvious picture?
   ① abstract art
   ② acrylic art
   ③ street art
   ④ cave art

13. What is a "mural"?
① a painting on canvas
② a painting on paper
③ a painting on wood
④ a painting on a building

14. What does "trompe l'oeil" mean?
① mistake of the eye
② picture on the ground
③ painting done with oils
④ moving picture

15. Why might a landscape artist write on his or her sketch?
① to instruct people how to draw it
② to make notes about how the scene looked
③ to prove the identity of the artist
④ to send it as a gift

16. Why do some artists choose to paint the original subject instead of using a photograph of the subject?
① They prefer to paint quickly.
② They prefer to capture the character of the subject.
③ They prefer to paint outdoors.
④ They prefer to move around while they paint.

17. What are the "primary colors"?
① black and white
② orange, green, and purple
③ red, blue, and yellow
④ brown and gray

18. What kind of paintings does the word "pentimento" describe?
   ① paintings which have been painted over a hundred years ago
   ② paintings which use rough strokes of a brush or palette knife
   ③ paintings which show that the artist has changed his or her mind during
      the process
   ④ paintings which are completely perfect in every way

19. Which of these does NOT damage paintings?
   ① darkness
   ② dust
   ③ chemicals
   ④ light

20. How does an art agent get paid?
   ① The artist pays the agent a fee each month.
   ② The gallery pays the agent for permission to hold an exhibition.
   ③ The agent receives a percentage of the money that the artist earns.
   ④ The buyers pay the agent a fixed amount for each painting they buy.

21. Which of these is NOT the job of an art critic?
   ① An art critic looks at art and thinks about how well it has been painted.
   ② An art critic gives his or her opinion about all kinds of artworks.
   ③ An art critic writes about art in magazines and newspapers.
   ④ An art critic paints pictures and displays them in galleries.

22. Why does Eli Broad lend his art collection to public galleries, museums, and
    universities?
   ① He wants lots of people to enjoy looking at the art.
   ② He wants everyone to know what a generous person he is.
   ③ He wants to make money from people paying to display his art.
   ④ He wants to avoid the cost of storing his huge collection.

23. Why did the old woman in Zaragoza decide to paint over the original fresco?

① She saw that the original painting was damaged.

② She didn't like the way Jesus' face had been painted.

③ She wanted to create a new tourist attraction.

④ She thought that she could do a better job than the original artist.

※ Choose the wrong part of each sentence. (24~25)

24.
이것은 세심한 생각을 요구하는데, 그냥 아무 방이나 되는 것이 아니기 때문이다.

→ This requires careful thought because not just any room will done.
   ①   ②   ③   ④

25.
이것은 반드시 물감이 완전히 마르도록 하기 위해서이다.

→ This is to making sure that the paint is completely dry.
  ① ② ③   ④

※ Choose each correct sentence that is translated into English. (26~27)

26.
그렇기 때문에 대부분의 동굴 벽화들은 빨간색, 검은색, 갈색, 또는 누르스름한 색이다.

① This is why most cave paintings are red, black, brown, or yellowish colors.

② This is what most cave paintings are red, black, brown, or yellowish colors.

③ This is that most cave paintings are red, black, brown, or yellowish colors.

④ This is how most cave paintings are red, black, brown, or yellowish colors.

27.

① While the restoration is carefully carried out, people might not like the result.

② If the restoration is carefully carried out, people might not like the result.

③ Even if the restoration is carefully carried out, people might not like the result.

④ Fortunately, the restoration is carefully carried out, people might not like the result.

※ Choose the correct word or phrase for each blank. (28~30)

28.

안타깝게도 많은 작가들은 세상을 떠난 후에야 비로소 유명해진다.

→ Sadly, many artists do not become famous ___________ after they are dead.

① so

② as

③ until

④ rather

29.

그렇지만 일단 그 화가가 강렬한 창작 욕구를 가지면, 그 여정이 시작될 수 있다.

→ But ___________ the artist has a strong desire to create, the journey may begin.

① until

② when

③ as

④ once

30.
물감의 거칠거칠한 질감은 마치 별들이 움직이고 빛나는 듯이 보이게 해 준다.

→ The rough texture of the paint makes it look ____________ the stars are
moving and shining.

① as though
② rather than
③ such as
④ unlikely

[Image Credit]

p.6   **Bisonte Magdaleniense negro**
By Museo de Altamira y D. Rodriguez [CC BY–SA 3.0 (http://creativecommons.org/licenses/by-sa/3.0)], via Wikimedia Commons

p.11   **A gallery in Tate Modern**
By Arpingstone [Public domain], via Wikimedia Commons

p.17   **Portrait of Henry VIII of England**
By Hans Holbein the Younger (1497/1498 – 1543) [Public domain], via Wikimedia Commons

p.25   **A still life painting**
By Jan Brueghel the Elder [Public domain], via Wikimedia Commons

p.26   *Mound of Butter*
By Antoine Vallon Antoine Vollon [Public domain], via Wikimedia Commons
L'Illustration horticole
By Lemaire, Charles Antoine (http://www.biodiversitylibrary.org/pageimage/92317) [Public domain], via Wikimedia Commons

p.27   *Guardian Spirit of the Waters*, 1878
By Odilon Redon [Public domain], via Wikimedia Commons
Mon portrait, 1867
By Odilon Redon [Public domain], via Wikimedia Commons

p.28   *Composition No 4*, 1911
By Wm M. Martin vasily kandinsky (http://masterpieceart.net/vasily–kandinsky/) [Public domain], via Wikimedia Commons

p.32   *Rat Photographer*
By Szater (Own work) [Public domain], via Wikimedia Commons

p.33   *Mona Lisa*
By Leonardo da Vinci [Public domain or Public domain], via Wikimedia Commons

p.36   *Jamaica Hut*
By William Berryman (Library of Congress[1]) [Public domain], via Wikimedia Commons

p.38   *Self–portrait*
By Vincent van Gogh [Public domain], via Wikimedia Commons

p.39   *The Starry Night*
By Vincent van Gogh [Public domain], via Wikimedia Commons

p.46   *The Painter's Studio*
By Joos van Craesbeeck [Public domain or Public domain], via Wikimedia Commons

p.47   **Studio floor used by Jackson Pollock at Pollock–Krasner House and Study Center in Springs, New York**
By Rhododendrites (Own work) [CC BY–SA 4.0 (http://creativecommons.org/licenses/by-sa/4.0)], via Wikimedia Commons

p.48   **Francis Bacon's studio at the City Gallery** *The Hugh Lane*, Dublin, Ireland
By antomoro (Own work) [FAL or FAL], via Wikimedia Commons

Sarah J. Dodd 선생님은…
현재 영국에 거주하시는 베테랑 초등 교사이자 작가이십니다. 호주에서도 수 년간 교직 생활을 하셨습니다. 과학 분야 박사
학위와 문예 창작 자격증을 가지고 계십니다. 대표 작품으로는 An Angel Anyway와 Little Angels 시리즈, The Lion Picture
Bible, Legs: the tale of a meerkat lost and found 등이 있습니다. 선생님의 동시가 시 선집 Let in the Stars에 수록되어
출간되기도 했습니다. 이외에도 유아들을 위한 그림책과 청소년들을 위한 소설을 집필하고 계십니다.

똑똑한 영어 읽기 Wise & Wide 6-10
그림에 관해 알아야 할 것들
Things to Know about Paintings

지은이 Sarah J. Dodd
펴낸이 정규도

초판 1쇄 인쇄 2017년 7월 7일
초판 1쇄 발행 2017년 7월 14일

편집장 최주연
책임편집 김명진, 최주연, 장경희, 박지영
표지·본문 디자인 이은희
전산편집 엘림
일러스트 이성희
번역 안창열

다락원 경기도 파주시 문발로 211
내용문의 (02)736-2031 내선 510
구입문의 (02)736-2031 내선 250~252
Fax (02)732-2037
출판등록 1977년 9월 16일 제300-1977-23호
Copyright © 2017, 다락원

ISBN 978-89-277-0431-7 18740 / 978-89-277-0371-6 18740(set)

http://www.darakwon.co.kr
다락원 홈페이지를 방문하시면 상세한 출판 정보와 함께 MP3 자료 등 다양한
어학 정보를 얻으실 수 있습니다.